THE KEYS OF
ROME

Louise Dale

Dragonheart
Publishing

Published in Great Britain in 2003
Dragonheart Publishing, The Grey House, Main Street,
Carlton-on Trent, Newark, Notts., NG23 6NW.

www.dragonheartpublishing.co.uk

British Library Cataloguing in Publication Data.
A catalogue record of this book is available from the British
Library.

ISBN 0 9543773 1 1

Cover painting by Ian R. Ward, Mansfield, Nottinghamshire.

The Time Trigger Series:
    The Curse of Rocamadour
    The Keys of Rome

Typesetting and production by
Richard Joseph Publishers Ltd, PO Box 15 Devon EX38 8ZJ

Printed in Great Britain by the Creative Print & Design
Group

For Richard

Contents

1

The Roman Coin

Through the swirling mists, a conquering army marched. The soldiers' boots struck the cobbles in their thousands. The column pierced the countryside in a straight line that stretched endlessly towards the Roman fort at Lindum, leaving behind the burning villages and murdered peoples of the ancient tribes of Britain. Alice could almost smell the stench of death. From her hiding place in the marshes, she saw the eagle on the standard at the head of the Roman Legion. And behind them trudged the slaves.

"No! No!" cried Alice.

"Wake up! Alice... Alice, wake up!"

"Help them... please!"

"Alice... WAKE UP!"

Robert was shaking her. He lifted her headphones.

"What group are you listening to, then?" he asked.

"Do you mind!" said Alice, opening her eyes. She snatched back the headset and replaced it in the pocket of the seat in front of her. "I was having a bad dream. Really bad. It was great at first. But then it was horrible."

"Nice and gory was it?" said Robert.

Alice scowled at him. She looked out of the cabin window and watched the toy houses growing. Soon, she could see washing lines slung from high-rise balconies filled with flowers and a train snaking along. It looked like *Legoland*. Now she could see pygmy people and battalions of tiny cars. They were coming down very fast and the buildings were getting bigger and closer.

"Urghhh! I hate it when planes land!" said Alice. She gripped the armrest.

"Bump! Bump! Bump!" teased Robert unkindly, as they felt the clunk of the aircraft wheels lowering beneath them.

"Shut up!"

"What? Alice Hemstock is scared?" said Robert sarcastically.

"I hate landing too!" said the shrill young voice of Robert's cousin from the seats behind.

"Sit back, Jessica! Is your seat belt still fastened?" asked Robert's mother.

At that moment, the aeroplane's wheels made contact with the runway and the engines thrust urgently backwards.

"Are we down?" whispered Alice.

"*Ladies and Gentlemen. Welcome to Rome!*" announced a member of the cabin crew over the loud speakers. "*For your safety, may I remind you to remain seated until the Captain has extinguished the seat belt signs and the aircraft has come to a complete standstill. The time in Rome is eleven thirty-five and the temperature this morning is a sizzling thirty degrees centigrade. On behalf of Captain Anderson and the crew, may I wish you a pleasant stay and a safe onward journey.*"

"Everybody all right?" said Robert's father, reaching up to find their hand luggage in the locker above. His chubby features were drawn into an affable smile.

"I am now," said Alice. "Do you think... "

"Come along Michael," said Robert's mother. "No time to chat. We need to find the platform for our train into the city. Pass me my coat!"

Mrs Felicity Davenport scowled impatiently at her husband over the rims of her glasses. Mr Davenport obediently lifted down the assortment of jackets and bags.

"Here you are dear," he said. "But if I were you I wouldn't wear that thick coat. It's..."

"Nonsense! I can hardly carry it, can I, with all these bags and children! And I do hope you can find us a taxi from the train to the hotel."

"Yes, please. I'm not walking!" added Jessica.

Robert and Alice exchanged looks and wisely decided not to speak. They nudged their way into the crowded aisle and headed for the exit. They emerged into the sweltering heat. Alice closed her mouth but the air only burnt her nostrils instead. She clattered down the steps after Robert.

"Mum looks like a fish," whispered Robert, looking at his mother. She had unwisely fastened her wool coat right up to its fur collar. Robert opened and closed his mouth mischievously.

"Come on then!" gasped Mrs Davenport and she swept away towards the terminal building.

Robert hauled his bag on to his shoulder. As he did so, the luggage label snagged the key ring on his belt and pulled it off. It skimmed across the ground with a tinkle. Alice jumped over it.

"Umm. Nice. Bet I know where you got it!" she said, stooping to retrieve it. She pushed aside the collection of modern keys to get a better look at the large coin that decorated the clip.

"Where then?" said Robert.

"In the gift shop at Lincoln Castle?" said Alice. "Last term, when we went with school... the day after that weird earthquake?"

"How did you know?" said Robert.

"Because I saw key rings like this one there. I remember them because the lady in the shop was complaining that all the small things had fallen and got mixed up when the building shook during the night. Do you remember?"

"Yeah! My bed shook," laughed Robert. "Dad thought a nuclear bomb had fallen on Nottingham, 'til we heard on the radio in the morning that it was the biggest earth tremor in England ever. Good job though... else I might not have found that!"

"The other key rings I saw weren't quite the same as this one," said Alice. "This is weird. If it's supposed to be a Roman coin, it's got funny markings on it. Roman coins usually have the profile of an emperor."

Alice shivered slightly, despite the heat. She suddenly felt a shadow of fear across her and glanced back over her shoulder. But all she could see were passengers swarming towards her. She looked at Robert.

"Do you... feel odd?" she said.

"Odd how?"

"Oh... never mind. Here... "

The strange feeling had passed. Alice shrugged and gave Robert the funny looking key ring. They wandered after the other passengers.

"I'm going to keep my eye out for some really good souvenirs on this holiday," said Alice. "This is Rome!"

Alice was desperate to see the Colosseum. And there were supposed to be genuine ancient Roman statues and pieces of columns just lying about the city for anybody to sit on.

Inside the baggage reclaim hall, Alice and Robert sat on luggage trolleys waiting for their suitcases to pop up through the flap on to the conveyor belt. Opposite was a series of wall posters. Each one had a different photograph of a painting or a sculpture with the name *Michelangelo* scrawled diagonally

10

across the bottom. Alice got up and walked along them.

"They remind me of the time I designed a Heathrow airport poster for a *Blue Peter* competition when I was about eight," Robert called over to her.

"Did you win?"

"Naah! It was a terrible painting of an aeroplane. Got a Blue Peter badge for entering though!"

"Cool!" said Alice. "I'd love to actually meet this Michelangelo guy."

"Why?" said Robert.

"Because I'd like to watch him painting," said Alice.

Robert gave Alice a funny look.

"It would be good to time travel again though," he said.

Alice's eyes glowed.

"Yes! Here in Rome!" she said. "But we'd need to find a Time Trigger, wouldn't we? Something connected to the past that will give us the power to time travel."

They were interrupted by a shout from Robert's dad.

"Over here, Rob!"

Robert and Alice helped Mr Davenport hoist the last of their cases on to their fleet of trolleys.

"Il passaporto, per favore," barked the man in a green uniform from behind the counter at the pass-port control. Alice and Robert hastily surrendered their passports.

"Looks like a Roman soldier," whispered Alice.

"Good job they don't still take Britons as slaves!" said Robert.

Alice shuddered, remembering her dream. The man stared intently at the two children.

"Grazie," he growled eventually and he pointed to

11

the metal detector, jabbering in Italian.

"Come on. We have to walk through," said Mr Davenport.

The guard nodded, pointing to their pockets. They dutifully tipped a jumble of hankies, coins, pens and bits of fluff into the plastic trays. Alice and Jessica went through first, followed by a stressed and hot looking Mrs Davenport.

To everyone's surprise, Robert triggered the alarm.

"Oh dear! Now what? Haven't you emptied your pockets Robert?" groaned his mother.

A guard took Robert to one side, lifted his arms and started running his hands up and down Robert's body. Alice giggled. Mrs Davenport glared at her. Alice's grin shrank into a scowl. "You're not my mum," Alice wanted to say. Just for a second, she almost wished Robert hadn't asked her to come to Rome with his family, while her own mother was working during the holidays. She was getting fed up with being ticked off. Robert's petite cousin didn't look as if she was going to be much fun either. Alice consoled herself with the thought that at least she was actually in Rome, even if it was only for three days.

The Italian customs man had reached the inside of Robert's thighs. Even Jessica tried to stifle a giggle. Robert's eyes looked like table tennis balls.

The man's hands stopped as he suddenly felt the key ring on the front of Robert's belt.

"Oops! Sorry! I forgot to unclip it," said Robert.

"Oh, Robert! Really!" huffed his mum.

The man examined the keys, hovering briefly over the big coin.

"It's only a child's toy, officer..." said Mr Davenport.

"*Si! Si!*" replied the official and he waved them all through.

"Tut! Tut! Been trying to smuggle antiques have

we?" smirked Jessica.

"Be quiet, Jess!" warned Robert crossly. He turned to Alice. "It's not a *toy* though!" he whispered. Then he stumbled slightly. "That aeroplane food wasn't great!" he said, suddenly rubbing his stomach.

For an instant, Alice felt queasy and sick too. She glanced at Robert. The last time she had experienced that particular kind of nausea was when they had time travelled back to the middle ages and met Richard the Lionheart. Thankfully, the odd feeling disappeared as quickly as it had come. But she breathed an uneasy sigh as she pushed her trolley out into the crowded airport terminal.

2

Taxi

The train whisked them speedily to the vast Termini station and they stepped out into the streets of Rome. It was a shock. The heat and the noise and the dirt and the crowds were a far cry from the subdued pace of their hometown of Newark.

All at once, they were descended on by half a dozen tall, brown Romans offering *"Tassi! Tassi!"*

Mrs Davenport's helpless air began to subside.

"Thank goodness! Yes, please..."

"Er, sorry. No!" interrupted her husband with uncharacteristic assertion. "Remember what the lady in the travel agency said? Proper taxi drivers don't tout for business. This lot will charge us a fortune."

"Fortune or not, Michael, I just want to get to the hotel. This heat is too much."

"My dear, why don't you take off your coat?" said Mr Davenport.

Robert suddenly shouted.

"Over there, Dad!" He had spied the official taxi rank.

"Well done, Rob! Come on everyone," said Mr Davenport.

With the cases, it was a tight squeeze in one taxi. Alice and Robert jumped into the back seat. Mrs Davenport got into the front passenger seat.

"I get car sick so I'll sit in the front seat... FRONT SEAT!" said Robert's mother to the taxi driver.

Alice fancied that the Roman looked scornfully at this English woman in a wool coat.

"I'm not sure that's such a good idea..." said Mr Davenport.

14

"Nonsense!"

"Why isn't it such a good idea?" asked Alice.

"You'll see!" replied Mr Davenport, squeezing next to Jessica in the back of the taxi. "Hotel Medici, *per favore.*"

A few seconds later they entered the frenzied race on the roads of Rome and Alice understood the warning. The cars and scooters vied madly for every centimetre of space. The taxi lurched and shunted, only just stopping behind the vehicle in front each time. The side streets were as bad as the main roads, with courageous pedestrians striding out, apparently intent on committing suicide but never quite succeeding. The little scooters were the worst.

"Don't Italians ever stop at red lights!" gasped Robert. "They accelerate when it goes red instead of braking!"

He nudged Alice to look at his mother. She was frozen with terror.

Alice smiled and looked out of the side window. She was spell bound. She relaxed her grip on the seat and saw for the first time, the awesome façades of this eternal city. The taxi veered around the Piazza della Republica and behind the Opera House and sped down the Via Nazionale. Hardly unable to decide which window to look out of, Alice gaped unashamedly at the opulent basilicas and palaces. With every new turn, she was greeted by a surprise even more fantastic than the last. Ornate marble fountains gave way to magnificent carved arches. And people and cars and scooters.

The taxi jarred to a halt with the smell of burning rubber. Mrs Davenport staggered through the sliding hotel doors leaving her husband to pay the driver.

The air-conditioning of the cool marble interior felt good.

"Here's your room key, Alice. Do take care of it," said Mrs Davenport. Jessica was about to protest. "No, Jessica. Alice is older. There's only one key for each room I'm afraid. Robert, you have your own of course."

Alice caught the smirk on Robert's face. She forced a smile at Jessica, hoping Robert's cousin didn't snore at night, or worse.

"Can we go out and explore?" said Alice.

"Good grief! Not yet. I need time to recover," said Mrs Davenport.

Robert's father saw the disappointment on the young peoples' faces.

"Surely they could go for a little walk... without crossing any roads, dear?" he said.

"Umm. I'm not sure about Jessica," said Mrs Davenport.

Robert looked as if he wasn't sure about having her with them either.

"Oh, please, Aunty Felicity. Please!" said Jessica, jumping up and down, making her blonde pony tail swish from side to side. "I'm only a bit younger than them."

"Two years, actually," said Robert unkindly.

"I'll be eleven soon... "

"All right, you two. That's enough!" Mrs Davenport looked hot and frustrated. "Just for ten minutes. Stay on this side of the road and come straight back. Have you got a map?"

"I have," said Alice, producing a guidebook from her bag. There was a folded city map in the back of the book.

"Ten minutes, that's all," warned Mr Davenport.

The three children slipped out through the sliding glass doors, back into the cloying heat. They walked to the corner of the street, past a bike and scooter hire shop and an Internet café. They were at the top of the steps next to the vast halls of Trajan's markets and towering above them, from the ruins of the Imperial Forum, was Trajan's column.

"Oh, wow!" gasped Alice.

Robert and Jessica gawped in silence.

"I can't believe it!" Alice leapt down the ancient steps and dodged round an elderly Roman woman sweeping litter. At the bottom of the steps they turned into the Piazza Venezia.

"It's fantastic! Look at all these ruined columns all over the place!" said Robert.

"It's more than fantastic!" said Alice. "Look at those fountains... and that palace... and those massive bronze chariots... and... " She had wheeled round and was looking straight down the Via dei Fori Imperiali. "... it's the Colosseum!"

"Wicked!" said Robert.

"Let's go and touch one of those columns," said Jessica. She skipped over and straddled the top, marking her pale shorts on the dirty white ridges.

Alice wandered across, trying to take in as much as she could of her new world. She ran her hand reverently along the cool structure.

"Hail, Caesar!" mocked Robert, standing on the fallen column behind his cousin.

"Is this where they had Vestal Virgins?" asked Jessica.

"Chariot races, more like," said Robert.

"That was in the Circus Maximus, I think. Just a minute. I'll look it up in my guide book... it's back in here somewhere... " Alice fumbled among the mess inside her little rucksack. "Here it is... "

Suddenly, Robert lost his footing and fell on to the parched grass beside the fallen column.

"Urgh! I don't feel too good," he said.

"Funny... neither do I," said Alice, gripping her stomach. Then she froze. "I think there's something going on, Rob," she whispered. "You know... like last term in France, on the school trip."

"You mean... we're going to time travel again? Then we must have found another Time Trigger, Alice. We can't travel without a Time Trigger... " He held up his hands in expectation, waiting for an answer.

Alice was nodding slowly.

"What are you two whispering about?" said Jessica.

Robert's eyes suddenly widened. Giving Alice a sideways glance, he unclipped his key ring and pointed at the funny looking Roman coin.

"Oops!" said Alice. But her blue eyes were sparkling.

3

Paper Trousers

"Do you still feel sick?" asked Robert, examining the coin.

"No. It's gone off. But I think something's going to happen, Rob, and I'm just a little bit scared."

"I'm not. We were all right last time."

"Only just!" said Alice.

"This time we might meet Julius Caesar!" hissed Robert, rubbing his hands together.

"What *are* you two talking about?" interrupted Jessica. "Can you include me in your conversation? I'll tell your mum you're leaving me out!"

Robert was about to retaliate with something unkind, but Alice glared at him.

"Come on, Jessica," she said. "Let's go back to the hotel now. We'll come back here later with your uncle and aunt. I'm starving. Maybe we'll get an ice-cream from one of these kiosks."

"Drink, more like," said Robert, trying to push his sticky blond hair from his forehead to put his sunglasses on.

They walked slowly up the steps. At the top, Alice turned to look back. Columns and arches and archaeological remains littered the cityscape for as far as she could see.

"What must it be like to live here?" she muttered to herself. "... amongst all this! This is not pictures in a book, or films, or stories. This is real. It's almost as if it happened last year ... Caesars and Roman legions. Kids like me ... lucky Roman kids ... they can touch all this history right next to them anytime they like."

She sighed deeply. "I wish we *could* time travel here." Her pulse quickened.

Back at the hotel, Robert's parents were in the foyer.

"About time!" said Mrs Davenport, who had changed into a cotton twin set and white trousers. "We've made a reservation at a *trattoria* that our next door neighbours recommended."

Robert's face brightened.

"We're not going in another taxi, are we?" asked Jessica in alarm.

"No, don't worry, dear," said Mr Davenport. "We'll be able to walk everywhere from now on."

"Phew!" said Jessica and Alice together.

They ambled through the crowded streets away from the ancient quarter of Rome, towards the more cosmopolitan city centre. Expensive boutiques mingled with Baroque churches in a confusion of historical opulence and modern glamour.

"We *are* going to go to the Colosseum aren't we?" said Alice.

"Of course. But not today," replied Mr Davenport. Alice wilted. "Felicity would like to go to the Vatican after lunch, wouldn't you, dear?"

Robert and Alice pulled disappointed faces at one another. Robert's mother didn't seem to be listening. She was admiring some *Versace* perfume in a shop window.

The restaurant was fun though. They ate wonderful fresh spaghetti in the cosy courtyard just off the pavement, watching the passing cocktail of tourists and elegant Romans. Mrs Davenport relaxed after a couple of glasses of red wine and everybody tucked into the spectacular ice-cream desserts.

"Good heavens, Michael! Look at the time!" said Mrs Davenport. "We need to get going or we won't have time to see inside St. Peter's!"

Alice and Robert groaned silently at one another again.

Half an hour later, they wound their way over the bridge across the River Tiber and along the approach to the Vatican City.

"Alice," said Jessica.

"Umm?"

"What exactly is the Vatican?"

Robert looked hopefully at Alice too.

"It's where the Pope lives. He's the head of the Roman Catholic Church," said Alice.

"Have you heard of the famous Sistine Chapel?" said Mr Davenport.

Both Jessica and Robert shrugged their shoulders, although Alice thought the name sounded familiar.

"That's where Michelangelo once covered the ceiling in beautiful paintings," said Mr Davenport.

"Aha!" said Alice, remembering the posters at the airport.

"Alice would like to go back in time and meet him face to face," said Robert, looking at Alice rather strangely.

He was wafting his key ring about behind his back so that only Alice could see it. She frowned at him. He was daring her to test the possible Time Trigger.

"Did Michelangelo paint the *Mona Lisa?*" said Jessica, trying to sound knowledgeable.

"No. That was another Renaissance artist called Leonardo da Vinci," said Robert's dad.

"When exactly was the Renaissance?" asked Alice, trying not to look at Robert.

"Hmm," said Mr Davenport, wiping his brow with his handkerchief. "I *think* it was during the Sixteenth Century."

"Do you mean in fifteen hundred and something . . .

like when the Tudors were around in England?" said Robert.

His dad nodded.

"Would you like to meet Henry the Eighth then, Alice?" said Robert dangerously.

"Or Elizabeth the First?" said Jessica, trying to join in.

Alice and Robert both looked at her. Robert stifled a giggle.

"William Shakespeare," said Alice suddenly.

"Oh. You'd like to meet him?" said Robert, waving the key ring around again.

"Yes. But not RIGHT NOW," said Alice rather deliberately through clenched teeth.

Towering above them, its mighty dome sparkling in the heat, was St. Peter's church, with the colossal statues of the apostles presiding over the fury of tourists in the square below.

"Cool church," said Robert. "Can we go inside?"

"That's the plan," said Mr Davenport.

"Oh dear. That official is saying something to Jessica... " said Mrs Davenport.

The man was talking in Italian to a slightly frightened looking Jessica and pointing to her legs.

"Oh, I think I know," said Robert. "You're not allowed to wear shorts in the church."

"*Grazie! Grazie!*" said Mr Davenport, signalling to the man that he understood.

"Now what?" said Robert. "We can't go in then, can we?"

Alice was looking around her. She saw a couple of young women with paper trouser things over their legs.

"Just a minute... " She bounded off towards a nearby souvenir shop that was tumbling with fake statues and trinkets. "Over here, Mr Davenport!"

she shouted. "You can buy these special paper trousers to cover your legs. Look!"

"Oh, yes! Excellent. Problem solved!" said Mr Davenport.

"I'm not wearing those!" shouted Jessica.

"If you don't, you'll have to wait outside," said Mrs Davenport.

Jessica looked as if she was going to cry.

"Loads of people are wearing them... cool people. Look... over there... and there," said Alice.

Jessica looked a bit calmer.

"Oh, all right. I haven't got much choice, have I? Why does it have to be me that looks an idiot?"

Robert was grinning unkindly at his cousin.

"Shut up, Robert!" said Jessica.

"I didn't say anything!" said Robert coyly. Jessica stuck her tongue out at him.

Inside the church, it was surprisingly quiet. The silence was peppered with the echoes of shoes and coughs. Visitors milled about everywhere and filed past the statue of St. Peter, touching a bronze foot worn smooth by the kiss of a million pilgrims.

"Dad, can Alice and I go off and explore on our own for a bit?" said Robert.

Alice looked at him suspiciously.

Mr Davenport glanced at his watch.

"Yes. I don't see why not. We'll meet you back here in half an hour. That OK?"

"Brilliant! Thanks, Dad! Come on, Alice," said Robert.

Before Jessica could notice, Robert and Alice slipped off in the direction of the dome. They paused by the entrance to the crypt.

"Might be real bones down there," said Alice. "It's the tomb."

For a second, Robert looked interested.

"Let's come back to that. Bet we won't be able to actually see anything. I want to climb the steps to the top of the dome."

Alice craned her neck. The mighty construction fanned out like a distant umbrella. She could see tourists the size of ants walking around an internal balcony.

"Look at those paintings on the inside of the dome. How do you think they managed to paint them all those years ago?"

"Dunno. Let's go and get a close up," said Robert.

They wandered outside and joined the queue for the lift to take them part of the way up. Even after the lift ride, they still had to climb hundreds of spiralling steps. There were warnings about the risk to people with weak hearts in several languages.

"Rob, I feel dizzy," puffed Alice as they finally emerged on to the internal balcony.

"You need to get fit."

"No. It's not that kind of feeling... "

"Oh, wow! We are SO high up!" said Robert, not really taking any notice of what Alice was trying to say.

He peered over the balcony at the tiny people on the ground so far below. Alice leant back against the wall. She still felt peculiar as she studied the wall next to her.

"Oh! Look!" she said. "I'd never have believed it... it's so clever. They're not paintings at all... they're mosaics! Thousands of tiny pieces of coloured stone. Close to, they don't look like much. But from a distance... from down there on the ground, they're faces and shapes. Oh, Robert. It's brilliant!"

"Yep... I've got to admit, that guy Michelwotsit was pretty clever."

"Hey, what's this?" said Alice suddenly. She was

still feeling very odd. "It isn't mosaic... oops! Oh, dear. I think I've just broken something." She looked furtively around.

"What have you done?" said Robert, grinning. "Naughty! Naughty! Let's have a look..."

They peered at the dusty object that had come loose from the wall. Alice rubbed it, trying to see more clearly.

"It's round. It's bigger than most of the other tiles. Hey... I think it's a coin of some sort. It's very like yours, actually" She staggered back again. "Oh, Rob... I feel really, really terrible..."

She turned to Robert. He had taken out his key ring. He looked different.

"You look weird, Rob. Almost see-through. I know... it's happening now..."

Robert was nodding.

"We're going to time travel," he said. "These things ARE Time Triggers. Quick! Take my hand!"

Alice closed her eyes. She recognised that amazing rush of feeling again, just like the last time they had time travelled. It felt like she was skate boarding over clear blue skies. It was freedom. With the thrill of a roller-coaster ride expanding inside her, she clung to Robert's hand and waited for the movement to slow down.

The next thing she knew, she was sitting on the floor of a more primitive wooden balcony, which swayed alarmingly alongside the half-decorated wall of the dome. The tourists and modern furnishings had vanished.

Somebody was looking down at them.

4

Vittoria

In the new gloom of flaming torch light, Alice could just make out the silhouette of a cloaked figure. A hood concealed the face but it was definitely looking straight at them. Then Alice noticed work-worn hands gripping long skirts beneath the cloak. It was a young woman. She was poised for retreat.

Robert slowly stood up, pulling on the handrail. The structure swayed unpleasantly like a rope bridge. He glanced below.

"Woah!" he said, retreating hastily from the edge.

At the sound of his voice, the young woman took a step back.

"No... don't go!" said Alice.

She edged to her feet with her back against the wall of the dome. In a glance, she saw that the walls were not fully decorated. Shiny new mosaic cubes about one centimetre square were heaped in wooden boxes against the wall. Tiles of the same colour were separated out, next to rulers, trowels and pots of glue.

Alice extended her hand towards the girl. "Please... who are you?"

"*When* are we?" added Robert. "I know *where* we are. We're still in the dome of St. Peter's. But we've gone back several centuries, at least."

There was something in their voices that interested the young woman. Wild green eyes glittered from the shadows of the hood.

"CH-O-W," Alice tried, smiling at the girl.

"*Arrivederci!*" nodded Robert.

The girl looked at him.

"That means good-bye, you idiot!" said Alice.

"Oops!" said Robert.

"*Ciao!*" Alice said again, trying to sound a bit more Italian.

A tiny smile crept across the girl's lips.

"*Buona sera,*" she replied quietly. "You... *inglese...* English?"

"Yes! Yes!... I mean *Si!* Oh dear, that's about all the Italian I know," said Alice.

"Don't look at me!" said Robert.

Suddenly, the young woman noticed the round piece of mosaic that Alice was still clutching. She started speaking to them in rapid Italian, pointing first at the odd looking tile in Alice's hand, then back down towards the entrance to St. Peter's. Alice shook her head in confusion.

"Do you know what this is?" she tried. "Is it a Time Trigger?"

Robert started demonstrating flying movements with his arms and twirled round, making the rickety platform wobble.

"Prat!" said Alice.

The girl was tugging on Alice's sleeve, pulling her towards the top of a very scary rope ladder that dropped down to another platform.

"You come help his... sister," she said, desperately trying to make them understand something.

"Whose sister?" said Alice.

But the girl pointed again at the long ladder.

"You have got to be kidding!" said Robert, assessing the distance and construction of the ladder.

"I don't think she is," said Alice. "She wants us to go down there."

The girl hitched up her skirt and swung herself over the edge on to the ladder.

"What d'ya think?" said Robert.

"Umm. I think... we have to give it a go," said Alice, doubtfully.

"Well, if she can do it in all those skirts, we ought to be able to!" said Robert.

"Yep. Let's go for it!" said Alice. She turned round and felt with her foot for the first rung. "Wish me luck!"

The next few minutes were some of the freakiest Alice could remember. The ladder was strongly made, and quite new, but it was a very long way down to the next platform and completely vertical. Alice had to look down every now and again, to avoid treading on the Italian girl's hands. And she was equally worried about Robert's size nine trainers edging down above her.

At the bottom, the girl waited for them. She pointed to another ladder and platform.

"Urgh! I need my travel sickness bracelets!" wailed Alice.

"Chicken!" sniggered Robert, slipping past her.

Alice shrugged and let him pass. At least she wouldn't have to worry about his big feet now.

They continued their descent using platforms and ladders until they reached a solid floor. The girl beckoned to them and they followed her through a doorway to a stone staircase that spiralled around the inside of the dome. It had hundreds of steps.

Alice slipped slightly.

"I don't like this," she said. "I wish she'd slow down. She's obviously used to all these steps. We're not."

They trudged on, round and round. Alice's back ached and her eyes were beginning to blur.

"Phew!" said Robert, as they emerged at ground level. "Do you have to do that every day?" he asked

the girl, forgetting that she didn't understand him.
The girl looked at him blankly.

"Oh, never mind!" puffed Robert. "Where to now?"

The girl seemed to understand that. She muttered
something and started off through a series of court-
yards around the Sistine Chapel, and down colonnaded corridors towards the perimeter of the
Vatican City. There was nobody about. Behind them,
a bell tolled, and men's voices echoed from inside one
of the chapels.

Suddenly, a man dressed in priest's robes scurried
across the path in front of them and the young woman ducked into the darkness behind one of the
columns. The man hurried on by, unaware of spying
eyes. Alice fancied that he couldn't see her or Robert
anyway.

On they went. At the sound of horses approaching,
the girl once more retreated to the shadows behind a
marble statue, beckoning urgently at the other two
to hide behind her. Two guards trotted past. Robert
looked as if he was about to dare to wave at one of
them.

"No!" hissed Alice.

Robert looked at her.

"Bet they can't see us," he whispered.

"She can!" replied Alice.

"Umm."

They both looked at their guide.

"What's your name?" said Alice. She looked at
Robert for help. "Come on Rob! What did your mum
say? Me keyamo Alice or something?"

"Could be ... sounds a bit familiar. Let me try. RO–
BERT," he said, pointing to his chest. "AL–ICE," he
said to the girl, pointing at Alice.

Alice winced. But the girl seemed to understand.
From beneath her hood she whispered something.

Robert looked as if he hadn't heard.

"*Mi chiamo Vittoria,*" she said again, in a musical Italian voice.

Robert offered her his hand.

"Very pleased to meet you, Vittoria," he said.

"What do you want us to do?" said Alice.

But with a brief smile, the Italian girl turned and continued along the outer corridor.

"We're going back towards the bridge across the River Tiber," said Alice.

"Yep," said Robert.

They hurried on into a sunset that silhouetted a different Roman skyline from the one that Alice remembered. They could smell the river quite a while before they reached it, and hear the gentle lapping of the water on the shore. Alice's feet squelched in the mud.

"Yuk! Hey ... where are you taking us?" she yelled ahead to Vittoria.

The girl had reached a small boat tied beneath the bridge. More people were nearby now, walking on the bridge above and talking or shouting. But nobody seemed to notice the three youngsters below.

"Rob... I'm not sure about this... " said Alice, hesitating. But Robert shrugged his shoulders and started to climb into the boat.

"Oh, come on. What choice do we have? We might time travel back to the Twenty First Century at any minute. By the way, have you still got that coin thing you pulled off?"

"Of course." Alice checked in her pocket and the funny round mosaic tile was wedged well down. With a reluctant sigh, she followed Robert into the boat.

The girl passed Robert an oar, which he took with a grin. Rather too enthusiastically, he started to paddle in the murky water. The boat rocked and bobbed as it floated out into the current.

"Gently, Rob!" called Alice, clutching the side of the tiny craft in alarm. "I don't want to get thrown into the River Tiber, like Romulus and Remus!"

Vittoria showed Robert how to strike the surface of the water slowly and deeply, and gradually he copied her rhythm. They floated down the inky river, using the current to give them more power and the oars to direct the boat away from the banks.

Before long, the girl tugged at Robert, pointing at the riverbank. By now, they had travelled quite a distance from the city centre. With difficulty, they managed to steer the little boat towards the bank until they felt the silt of the riverbed beneath them. Hitching up her skirts once more, the young woman jumped out. Frowning at the stench and goo of the mud, Alice copied her, closely followed by Robert. They hauled the boat out of the water.

Once again, the English children followed their guide, this time towards the steps of what looked like a church. Alice and Robert squelched behind in their wet trainers. Vittoria looked nervously around her before opening the creaky doors. It was pitch black inside. They went in. Alice bumped into Robert as he stopped suddenly. Vittoria was crouching in the darkness, feeling on the floor for something. She located what she was looking for and pulled.

"It's a trap door!" hissed Robert over his shoulder at Alice. As the wooden covering lifted, they could see a golden, flickering glow of torchlight and a flight of wooden steps descending below.

"Oh, no! What now?" whispered Alice.

One at a time, they climbed down and waited for their eyes to adjust. Vittoria took the flaming torch from the wall. They were in some kind of entrance chamber. There were cobwebs everywhere. In front and on either side, narrow tunnels extended away from them, dug beneath the outskirts of Rome. Alice could see little cubicles cut four high, one above the other, all along the tunnels.

"Robert," she said nervously. "These are graves. I think I know where we are... "

"Well... where are we then?"

"The Catacombs of Rome," said Alice, shivering.

5

Catacombs and Vagabonds

Robert whistled.

"Cool," he said, his eyes glinting in the gloaming. "For a load of dead bodies, these don't smell too bad. Must be skeletons by now." He breathed into Alice's ear and ran his fingers up her back, before setting off after Vittoria.

"Shut up!" called Alice.

She shuffled past the tombs of long dead Christians. Most were sealed with stones, a few with marble. The odd one had only a fabric curtain concealing the remains within. There were inscriptions on some of the stones. Alice would have liked to stop and look at those, but she had no intention of being left here alone.

It wasn't long before the tunnel widened into a hallway with more passages leading off on all sides. Vittoria took a new tunnel on the left, then veered sharply right past endless burial cells, until she came to what appeared to be a dead end, sealed by a rock. She took a few steps to one side and reached into a small hole. To Alice's surprise, the wall started to slide back. The heavy stone grated and jarred on the uneven floor and Alice could hear the turning sound of a mechanical device. Beyond was a secret chamber.

"Wicked!" murmured Robert.

The Italian girl drew her cloak around her and squeezed through the opening. Alice followed.

The dingy cave was home to dozens of people. But nobody looked at them. Somebody somewhere was moaning.

"Can they see us?" asked Robert.

"I don't think so," said Alice.

They stepped quite close to one group. They were young people, probably teenagers. They were thin and raggedly dressed and stared miserably into the air. One youth slowly wiped a blade along a dirty cloth, trying to polish it. Robert wiggled his head and looked straight at them, bulging his eyes deliberately. There was no response from the group. To these people, at least, Robert and Alice were invisible. But not to Vittoria. She tugged Robert's arm and motioned towards a far corner.

"Michelangelo... " she muttered.

Both Robert and Alice looked sharply at her.

"Did she say *Michelangelo?*" said Robert.

Alice nodded and frowned.

They made their way between the huddled groups towards a corner where a man sat with his back to them, drawing on the floor with charcoal. Smudged sketches sprawled across the walls around him. He looked up as Vittoria touched his shoulder. Then he saw Robert and Alice. He threw down the charcoal stick and stood up to face them. He was a tall young man, probably in his late teens. His curly hair was tied loosely behind him. His long overcoat brushed the floor. It was torn and dirty. He rubbed his moustache and goatee beard with blackened fingers as Vittoria spoke excitedly to him in a cascade of animated Italian. He straightened his shoulders and his eyes widened as he listened to her.

"*He* can definitely see us," said Robert quietly.

Vittoria fell silent. Nobody spoke. A fire crackled and spat behind them. What little fresh air there was seeped in through the crevices high above them but Alice wrinkled her nose at the unpleasant smell of unwashed bodies.

"Sit. Please," said the young man, eventually.

"You speak English?" said Robert in surprise.

"Yes. I have travelled and learned the language of the Britons of your time," said the man.

Alice frowned at him. It was a strange thing to say.

"You have a key... another key?" the young man continued.

Alice shook her head.

"We have no keys... " she said.

"*Si. Si,*" interrupted Vittoria, nodding. She pointed at Alice's pocket.

Then Alice understood. She brought out the mosaic coin.

"Do you mean this?"

The man nodded enthusiastically.

"Do you have another one, too?" he said.

" I don't, but Robert... "

"Just a minute," interrupted Robert. "Who are you? And how did you know about the coins... or- *keys*... or whatever they are?"

The two young men looked at each other. Alice could feel Robert's muscles tensing beside her and she could see the aggression in the eyes of the older boy.

"You have been brought here by the spirits of time to help me, my friends," said the young man. "And there is much to do."

"You don't sound Italian," said Alice.

"Ha! Me? A Roman?" The young man laughed unpleasantly.

"But she called you Michelangelo," said Robert.

"What of it?" said the man.

"Well the Michelangelo who built that dome and did all those paintings... well... he was Italian I thought?" Robert looked at Alice for support.

For a moment, the young man looked confused.

Then he seemed to understand their mistake.

"No, no! Not Michelangelo *Buonarroti!*" He laughed again and spoke in Italian to Vittoria, whose eyes wrinkled with humour.

"I am not *that* Michelangelo. *He* died twenty years ago, the miserable old fool!" He saw the surprise on Alice's face. "Oh, he may have been a damn fine painter, I'm not saying he wasn't. But, well... " He looked fondly at Vittoria. "Let's just say he was a bit grumpy. Mind you, I don't blame him... he had to put up with a lot from Pope Julius, always changing his mind about the design of St. Peter's. But he could have looked after his own a bit better." Again he looked at Vittoria, who withdrew further under the large hood. Alice realised she had not yet seen the girl's face properly.

The young man stood up and gave them a flourishing bow.

"Michelangelo Merisi da Caravaggio at your service," he said. "Well that's what most people think! Now that you have come at last, we must plan how to use a Time Trigger to rescue my sister."

Robert and Alice exchanged excited glances.

"Where is your sister?" asked Alice.

"Trapped back with the Caesars, my friends."

Alice gasped.

The young man nodded.

"Without one of the Time Triggers, she cannot escape. You must help her."

At that moment, Alice, who was still holding the round piece of mosaic, gripped her stomach. Robert squinted at her.

"You O.K?"

Alice shook her head.

"I think we're about to time travel," she whispered.

"What... uh,oh! Yes. I feel it too," said Robert.

Robert grasped Alice's outstretched hand. "*Arrivederci*" he said.

"No!" shouted the young man. "Not yet! We have not begun to... "

Alice watched as Vittoria and the older boy faded behind a thickening veil of ripples. She closed her eyes to try to reduce the vertigo. In an age of seconds, they were somewhere else. They had time travelled again.

It was cold and the silence was absolute. Alice opened her eyes but darkness remained.

"Rob! Where are you?"

"Over here! Keep talking... I'll find you."

"Where are we Rob? Rob?"

"Keep talking... oh, there you are."

They backed into one another.

"Hang on... I know it's somewhere... " said Robert. "Ah, ha!"

A tiny blue ray of light flickered into their world.

"Phew!" said Alice.

"It's on my pen knife. Thought it might be useful one day," said Robert.

His face looked rather sinister, lit from beneath by the azure beam. He pointed the little torch away from them and went over to investigate. Alice recognised the rough walls.

"We're still in that secret chamber at the end of the catacombs. Oh, Rob! We're sealed in!"

6

The Pantomime Policeman

"**O**.K. Let's think," said Robert. "If we follow the wall round we should come to the door."

"Then what?"

"Hang on. Give me a chance. Do I detect panic, Alice?"

Alice thumped him. She could feel Robert sniggering.

"Your time will come," she retaliated.

"Yes, I should think it will. Sooner rather than later, at this rate." Alice could see Robert's ghostly hands sweeping the walls in the torchlight. "On the other hand... maybe not!"

His fingers disappeared into a small hollow. Alice shuddered at the thought of hidden beasties inside.

"Aha!" Robert pulled on something. "A lever! Bit stuck though... "

Then suddenly, the lever released, sending Robert crashing back into Alice and they both fell on to the floor.

"Ow! That hurt!" said Alice, rubbing her leg.

"Worth a little pain though... "

Sure enough, the stone door was very slowly grinding open. Yellow light flooded through. The turning mechanism creaked and wailed.

"Phew!" said Alice.

Then, to her dismay, it fell silent again. The door was jammed.

"Oh, no!" groaned Robert.

But there was a thin gap. Alice jumped to her feet and started to squeeze herself through the opening.

Her top ripped across her shoulder blades but she forced herself out into the brightness beyond. Robert tried to follow.

"Oh! Help, Alice. I think I'm stuck! Pull me through!"

Just for a second, Alice hesitated. Revenge warmed inside her and she smirked at Robert, crossing her arms to annoy him.

"Al–ice! Please!"

She shrugged her shoulders, and sauntered back. Taking Robert's arm and putting one foot up on the wall to steady herself, she pulled as hard as she could. With a ripping sound, Robert was delivered into the catacomb tunnel. He screwed up his eyes reproachfully at Alice, then grinned and felt the back of his combat trousers.

"Oops! No pocket. Mum's going to shout," he said, cringing.

They looked around them. The tunnel was now lit by electric lights and instead of the curtains and marble covers they had seen on their way in, the burial cells were open and empty.

They started to retrace their steps towards the entrance of the catacombs, remembering to turn left and then right in reverse. Alice was thinking. They had entered these ancient excavations in the Sixteenth Century and now they were leaving them in the Twenty First Century.

"We are at the latest point in time right now, aren't we?"

Robert looked back at her with raised eyebrows.

"What I mean is, now is as late as it gets, isn't it?" she said.

"Well, now is a bit later than it just was. And now is a bit later again. And now . . . "

"Yes, all right!" said Alice. "But what I'm thinking

is... well... do you think we could travel forwards too, into the future, as well as backwards to the past?"

Robert was more serious now. He considered the problem.

"Not sure I want to try," he said. "... might evaporate into thin air."

Alice nodded thoughtfully.

They were almost out. The entrance had changed too. There were permanent steps now, instead of the rickety old wooden ladder that had been used in earlier times. Robert cautiously opened the door. The furniture in the church interior was modern, but the decorated walls looked old and original.

"Sshh!" whispered Robert. They peered round a pillar. A man sat behind a pay counter, reading a newspaper. A radio blared from the shelf behind him.

"Uh, oh! Looks like you need a ticket these days. We haven't paid, have we? How are we going to get past *him*?" whispered Alice.

"Shall we make a run for it?" said Robert.

"Look!" said Alice, pointing into a rubbish bin. "Old tickets!"

They looked at each other and grinned. Robert reached in and retrieved two crumpled tickets. He smoothed them out on his knee.

"Perfect," he said. "It's the wrong date on them... but if we're quick, he won't notice. Ready?"

"Yep," said Alice.

They boldly stepped out into the sunny courtyard and strolled casually towards the counter.

Without stopping, Robert put the tickets on the edge of the counter, giving the man a cheesy grin. Alice followed close behind and smiled a big smile, before breaking into a run towards the exit. She caught a glimpse of the man examining the tickets out of the corner of her eye as they raced out into street as fast as they could. Alice heard the man's angry shouts fading as they turned the corner and kept on running. They dodged a Roman businessman who almost dropped his briefcase and Alice had to step off the curb to avoid two elderly ladies. She jumped at a loud hooter. A woman in high heels perching on a scooter zoomed past.

At the corner of a big road that crossed the river, they stopped, laughing and panting at the same time.

"I think I know where we are," said Robert, recovering his breath at last. "That's the big dome, look."

They had run quite a long way back and were once again close to the entrance of the Vatican City.

"That was some adventure!" breathed Alice. "And now we know we have a time travelling quest. It's something to do with that Michelangelo's sister who needs rescuing from a Roman Caesar."

Robert grinned broadly.

"I suppose we'll just have to time travel back to Ancient Rome then," he said.

"The trouble is ... " said Alice. " ... we don't know enough yet. Which Roman Caesar? And who is that guy's sister?"

"Umm. I see what you mean," said Robert. He looked down at the Time Trigger coin in his hand. "Presumably these Triggers will take us back again, won't they?"

"Yes. I think they will," said Alice. "But hopefully not right now, or your mum will kill us!"

"Come on, then!" said Robert.

A few streets further on, they turned to walk down the approach to St. Peter's Square. They joined the throngs of tourists strolling past the Vatican Post Office and the curved colonnades and made their way across the square to one of the enormous bronze portals at the top of the steps.

Alice spotted Robert's parents. Jessica scowled at them. Alice knew she was cross because they had gone off without her.

"Thank goodness!" said Mrs Davenport. "Robert, your father said half an hour ... "

"Sorry! Sorry!" said Robert. "What have you three been doing then?" He was trying to change the subject rather too obviously.

"Waiting for you mostly!" replied his mother crossly. "Good grief! What on earth have you done to your top, Alice? You are both absolutely filthy!"

Robert clamped his hand over his missing pocket and took a few steps back.

"Umm ... well ... it was very dirty up in the dome," he said.

"O.K. everyone. Let's try not to have a big row here," said Mr Davenport. "I suggest we make tracks back into the city and look for a nice place to eat. What do you say?"

Everyone looked at each other a bit sheepishly. But the mention of food had calmed the atmosphere a little. Jessica was still glaring at her cousin though, and she stubbornly walked between Robert and Alice all the way back across the river. Alice would really have liked to talk more to Robert about their adventure back in time, in particular about the identities of Michelangelo and Vittoria, but she didn't want to risk causing any more trouble.

She was getting accustomed to the chaos of Rome as they meandered along the noisy streets, passing dozens of ancient buildings mixed in with modern restaurants and offices.

They rounded the corner of Via del Corso.

"Oh, a café! I'm really thirsty. Can we stop Aunty

Felicity? Please?" whined Jessica.

Mrs Davenport surveyed the plateau of little tables that almost blocked the entire pavement. There were two empty tables in the middle.

"Looks nice, dear?" said Mr Davenport optimistically.

"Yes. All right... "

Before she could change her mind, the three children squeezed through and sat down.

Although it was early evening, it was still very hot and Robert's parents both looked pleased at the thought of something to drink.

"My feet are killing me!" said Jessica.

Alice looked down at the younger girl's trendy wedged sandals. She was glad of the rest too, and her feet were feeling rather sweaty in trainers. Robert pulled at her sleeve and pointed into the road in front of them. He was laughing. Alice looked at the grand palace that overlooked the Piazza Venezia. The mighty bronze statues on the roof looked impossibly heavy to have somehow been lifted up so high. But such glories now seemed commonplace even after only a few hours in this amazing city, so why was Robert so amused? Then she saw him.

Standing on a round podium right in the middle of the road was a Roman policeman. He was splendidly dressed in a glowing white uniform crowned by a gilded dome of a hat and on his hands he wore oversized white gloves that reminded Alice of Mickey Mouse. He was directing the crossroads of throbbing traffic that attacked him, five lanes wide at the mouth of some roads. His graceful arms danced in deliberate rhythms as he bewitched his attackers into obedience. Alice was mesmerized.

If a car or scooter tried to sneak past him, he pointed assertively at them and directed them around a way they did not want to go, as punishment for their impudence. Not a single vehicle was able to defy him. His power was such that with his upheld arm, he could hold back the urgent grunting of a line of a dozen scooters, only slowly lowering the arm to release them in an impatient roar when he was satisfied that they had waited long enough. All the time, he smiled courteously with his mouth, but snarled with his eyes.

A handsome waiter delivered a tray of fantastic looking bottles to their table.

"Great!" said Alice.

Robert was still transfixed by the policeman's show.

"Cool cop!" said Robert.

"What happens when he gets tired, or needs to go to the loo?" giggled Jessica. "Oh. That reminds me. Aunty Felicity... "

Jessica went off with her aunt in search of the toilets and at last, Alice and Robert had a chance to talk.

7

𝕽oller 𝕭oots

"**A**ny ideas who he was then, our friend in the catacombs?" said Robert.

"Well, not THE Michelangelo, obviously," said Alice.

"But he must have known him."

"Or she did, the mysterious Vittoria. They knew about the coins, didn't they? He knew there was another one."

"And they could see us, so they must be time travellers too."

"Mmm. But why stick it in amongst the mosaic? Why didn't he go back and rescue his own sister?"

"Dunno. Odd isn't it. Hey, anyone would think we were experts! We've only done this once before," said Robert. "Maybe that earthquake happened in Lincoln so I would see my coin in the castle gift shop and buy it. Where's yours, Alice? Let's have another look."

Alice looked at him. "You could be right about the earth tremor ... "

"Don't be silly, I was only kidding."

But Alice wasn't.

She put her coin on her knee under the table, like Robert, and they examined them again.

"They called them *keys*, remember?" said Alice.

"Funny looking keys," said Robert.

"Keys to what?" said Alice. "And what about his sister being trapped or captured by Caesars ... that's even further back in time. Presumably they did travel back at one point?"

"Unless . . . ' Robert looked at Alice, but she already knew what he was about to say.

"Unless they travelled FORWARDS," she said excitedly.

"Sshh! She's coming back," said Robert, forcing a smile at his cousin.

They made conversation about foreign toilets. But Alice was trying to remember everything, in case there was a clue she had missed. Why would Michelangelo and Vittoria need Alice and Robert? Maybe they wanted another coin. Maybe they had lost their time travelling powers somehow. And how were the two coins connected? If they belonged together, how did they get separated? Robert had bought his in Lincoln, but she had found hers in Rome. She was distracted from her thinking by Mr Davenport.

"Anyone fancy a visit to the Roman Forum? It's just over there. Before we find a restaurant. It says in my guide book that most of it is open now and we ought to see as much as we can, since we're only here for two more days."

Everyone nodded.

"Can we have a quick look in that souvenir shop on the way past?" said Jessica.

"Already?" said Mrs Davenport.

"Please. I've brought my money." Jessica was whining again.

"Wouldn't mind half of what she's got in that purse," said Robert under his breath. "Her parents give her loads of spending money. It's not fair."

"I'd like a look in the shop though. Look at those roller blades and skate boards!" said Alice.

"Two minutes only, then," said Mrs Davenport.

They entered the shop. Alice went straight over to the magnificent selection of roller blades. There was a particularly interesting pair of roller boots that had two special wheels that could fold away into spaces in the soles, converting them back into ordinary trainer boots.

"Mr Davenport. How much are these?" she asked.

"Let me see, dear," said Robert's dad. "Umm. I think this many euros converts to about fifteen pounds."

"Oh. Thanks," said Alice, trying not to sound too disappointed.

She'd brought all the rest of her Christmas money with her, as well as the spending money her mum had given her, but fifteen pounds still sounded a lot.

"How much do you have, dear?" said Mr Davenport.

"I'm not sure," said Alice. She knew she was on dodgy ground now. Working out money and telling the time still sometimes got her confused. She might be top in music, art and history, but maths was definitely not her strong point.

"Show me," said Mr Davenport kindly.

Alice tipped out the contents of her purse into her hand. Mr Davenport had a quick look.

"Well... you've got nearly fifty euros here, young lady. That's about thirty English pounds, roughly. So the skates would take about half of your money."

Alice looked more hopeful.

"Cool," said Robert joining them. "That's much less than you'd pay back home, you know."

"Is it?" said Alice. "And I'd still have quite a bit left to buy other things?"

"Yes. I think so," said Mr Davenport. "If you want them, I should buy them now. I doubt we'll get the chance to come back this way again."

Alice made up her mind. She tried one on to make sure she had the right size, then took them over to the counter and paid for them.

Robert didn't see anything he fancied, although he showed Alice a collection of gladiator models.

"Bit grisly, aren't they?" said Alice.

"I'm gonna wait until we go to the Colosseum tomorrow to get something there," he said. "Hey! D'ya think we could use the coins to go back to Ancient Rome and see real gladiators and stuff?"

"Not sure I want to," said Alice. "We might end up the wrong side of the lions!"

Robert laughed enthusiastically, making snarling noises at Alice.

"You are *so* not cool, Rob," she said. "Hey, where's your mum and dear little Jessica?"

"They went next door to the perfume shop," said Mr Davenport. "Everybody all done here? Shall we wait outside?"

Mr Davenport held the door and they exchanged the air conditioning of the shop for the heat of the Roman streets. Thankfully, the other two were just coming out of the perfume shop, both clutching posh carrier bags.

"You'll smell nice, then," said Robert to his cousin.

She frowned at him, not sure whether he was teasing or not.

"Would you like to try some back at the hotel, Alice?" said Jessica, pulling a column shaped glass bottle from her bag.

"O.K," said Alice. It would keep the peace at any rate. She looked down at the bag containing her new roller boots and smiled to herself. She couldn't wait to try them out.

For the next half an hour, they strolled around the fallen remains of the Roman Fora. The clover covered steps and decaying stumps of once great columns provided a welcome oasis from the noise and dirt of the modern city around them. Alice tried to imagine the glory of the temples with swaggering senators on the steps. This was once the powerhouse of an empire, but an empire that she knew was famous for its murders and slavery.

Robert joined her.

"Are you thinking what I'm thinking?" he said.

"Doubt it."

"Bet you are," said Robert.

"What am I thinking then?"

"Bet you'd like to try and use the coins to go back to *this* Rome," whispered Robert eagerly.

Alice took out the coin from her pocket and looked at it. Would she like to? It could be dangerous. But what an opportunity!

"It's probably our destiny, anyway," she murmured.

She looked around. Robert's parents and Jessica were quite a long way off. Maybe... just maybe...

But Robert was already taking her arm. His eyes were shut and he had his coin key ring in the other hand.

8

The Murdered Caesar

Alice felt the intense energy of a turbulent disturbance in the space and time around them that was propelling them back to an unknown destination. Wind and heat brushed her body, but slowly, the powerful feelings started to subside. She peeped through half shut eyes and began to absorb her surroundings. She could not stop herself from gaping hopelessly at what she saw. She *was* here. They really were back in Ancient Rome.

She listened to the noises and noticed the smells. Ox carts clattered over the cobbles, driven by merchants on their way to and from the vast markets. A group of centurions walked past, wearing red and gold cloaks and plumed helmets. They were deep in animated discussion, obviously excited about some battle conquest. Alice shivered. She wondered whether the victory had been at war or at the gladiator games. A woman scolded her children, whose marbles had rolled too close to the soldiers' sandals. Further away, two barefoot young men with rope collars were humping sacks on to the back of a cart, watched by an elegant couple wearing the white tunics of Roman Citizens. The woman had many gold and silver necklaces and bracelets, and delicate beaded earrings. Her elaborately curled hair was pinned back with beautiful combs. When the sacks were loaded, the man helped his wife on to the seat at the front of the cart. Then he climbed up himself and whipped the horse on. The two young men trotted behind.

"Slaves," murmured Alice.

When the dust from the cart settled, Alice could see some officials standing on the temple steps across the street. They wore white togas with a purple stripe. Magnificent buildings towered around her, shimmering in the heat.

"Let's have a look around," said Robert excitedly. Alice climbed the steps behind Robert, still holding the carrier bag with her new skate boots and they entered the cool marble interior of the palace. Footsteps approached from a side aisle. There was no time to hide. Alice held her breath. Robert looked as if he was trying to blend in with the mosaic scene behind him.

Thankfully, it seemed as if they were invisible. Two more officials in togas walked past.

"Do you think they're Senators?" whispered Robert.

"Maybe," said Alice.

They cautiously tiptoed further in, past mosaic walls and statues of gods. They walked through to an inner courtyard. In the centre, the sound of trickling water in the fountain made Alice thirsty again. On the other side of the courtyard was a doorway, guarded by two sentries.

At that moment, the doors swung open. Robert and Alice ducked behind the fountain. An older woman breezed through, followed by four younger women with veiled faces. Alice peeped out. She retreated hastily as she saw a slight movement from beneath the veil of the last girl.

"Was she looking at us?" said Alice, when they had gone.

"Who?"

"That last one. I think I saw her eyes. I think she could see us."

"She didn't do anything. Mind you, neither would I if I had that first one for a teacher! Miss Walton, our

French teacher back home, is a pussycat compared!"

Alice nodded.

Just then, someone wailed loudly from inside the villa. The sentries drew their swords, turned and plunged through the doors, leaving them wide open. Robert and Alice looked at one another.

"Well?" whispered Robert, glancing across to the doorway. "Shall we?"

Alice nodded and they crept through the portal to investigate.

The inside of the villa was sumptuously decorated. Elegant cushioned couches surrounded low tables laid with olives, bread, mushrooms and fish and several discarded silver and bronze goblets. Through an archway beyond, Alice could see steps leading down to the waters of a decorated Roman bath. For an instant, she thought she saw the shadow of someone else reflected in the water.

In the centre of the floor in front of them, a boy was hunched over the limp body of a middle-aged man with a crippled arm. The dead man's toga was purple. Alice thought she could just make out one word that she understood amongst the guards' mutterings.

"He said *Caesar*... didn't he?"

As she spoke, the young man turned. He had heard her. He sprang up, adjusting the belt of his white tunic. The leather of his sandals squeaked on the marble floor as he stepped towards them.

"U-oh! Trouble!" said Robert.

The boy nodded a greeting, as if he already knew them. But his face was creased in hatred.

"You are too late," he spat. He spoke in broken English with a heavy accent. "Agrippina and Nero have succeeded. My father is dead!"

"Who are you?" said Robert.

"What do you mean? Are you playing games with

me? You know exactly who I am! We met yesterday at the chariot race! But yesterday, my father was alive! I told you my stepmother would murder him if you did not give me one of the keys. Now she will try and murder me!"

"Hang on... what do you mean we met *yesterday?*" said Robert.

The other boy's eyes bulged with anger.

"You time travelled here yesterday to rescue that Briton slave girl!" he said.

"I think I know what's happening," said Alice. "I bet we're *going* to travel back to before now. In our future, we will travel back to this boy's past."

"You mean if we travel slightly further back in time... to yesterday... the next time we time travel?" said Robert.

"Exactly!" said Alice.

"Stop whispering!" said the Roman boy. "You shall NOT have her back, unless you give me a key!"

"He's a time traveller!" said Robert.

Suddenly, Alice tripped. She struggled to keep her balance but her shoelace was caught beneath the leg of a table. Her ankle twisted painfully and she sank to the floor. She tugged and pulled but the lace was stuck fast.

"Get up, Alice! Now!" shouted Robert.

"I'm trying to," she said.

She kicked the table hard with her other leg. The table still did not move but something soft fell from a hiding place underneath it and plopped to the ground. It was a small pouch.

The Roman boy gasped. He seemed to recognise it.

"I thought my father had only one," he said.

Instinctively, Alice reached across and picked up the pouch.

"No! That one is mine!" screamed the boy.

Then he turned to the guards and shouted something in Latin. They looked at him strangely and hesitated. Alice knew that the guards couldn't see her. But she knew that she was in great danger. She wrenched her foot free from her trapped trainer and pushed the little pouch into a pocket. Alice kicked off the other trainer and snatched her new roller boots from the carrier bag. She shoved her feet inside, yanking the laces as tight as she could in one big pull and stuffed them inside the boots.

The guards started to advance blindly, slashing into the air with their swords.

"Bah!" cried the Roman boy, frustrated by the futile actions of the soldiers.

He seized one of their swords and lunged towards Alice. She rolled over just in time as the sharp blade crashed down on the floor making a fountain of sparks.

"Alice, run!" yelled Robert. He grabbed a small table, sending the serving vessels and jugs crashing on to the floor. He hurled it at the boy, giving Alice a chance to escape into the decorated Roman bathroom.

Robert backed through the doorway, stalked by the other boy.

"Split up!" he hissed at Alice.

Robert ran one way around the fragrant pool and Alice went the other. The boy hesitated, but a moment later Alice heard his sandalled feet on the poolside some way behind her.

Robert was shouting something. She glanced over, and to her horror, Alice saw that he was shimmering and fading. Then he disappeared completely. Robert had escaped by time travelling.

"But... I'm still here!" she breathed.

9

ℌizza

𝔄 lice kept on running. She groped in one of her trouser pockets, feeling for her Time Trigger as she ran. It was the wrong pocket. The footsteps behind her were getting closer with every pace. The two guards stood in the doorway to the chamber where the dead emperor lay, blocking her escape. They gawped at the Roman boy chasing no one with his sword. Alice had almost completely circumnavigated the bathing pool and the young Roman was gaining on her. There was nowhere else to go.

She barged at the two guards. The surprise was enough. They fell backwards with the sudden force of the invisible assault and she plunged between them. Luckily for her, as they tried to stand up, the boy crashed into them again. He fell into the heap of flailing limbs. Trying to ignore his angry shouts, Alice bent down and flicked out the wheels of her roller boots.

She skated back through the inner courtyard and straight down the middle of the huge palace vestibule. The marble floor was a skater's dream, apart from the slightly knobbly bits when she rolled over a mosaic. She roller-skated on, fumbling in her pockets for the old coin. She found it and smiled. She almost wished she had her personal CD player. A little music would be good to skate to. She gripped the coin tightly.

With her heart pounding and her hair streaming behind her, she shot out of the entrance. Then she saw the steps.

"Oh, nooo ... !"

At the top of the steps she lost control and flew upwards, closing her eyes in the rush of air, waiting for the smash. But to her amazement, the pain in her knees was not too bad. She knelt on the soft grass in the evening twilight, panting furiously. Robert was grinning down at her.

She brushed her long hair from her face and took a long, deep breath. Then she burst into laughter.

"Wicked!" she said. "A bit close though... he nearly got me!"

"You used the skates then," said Robert, pointing to the scuffed wheels.

Alice nodded, snapping the wheels back into the soles of the boots.

"My old trainers are back in Ancient Rome," she said. "How cool is that?"

They both laughed.

"Hey! We time travelled separately," said Alice. "We've never done that before."

"Yeah. When we time travelled in France, we seemed to need both halves of the Time Trigger stone."

"That's it!" said Alice. "They were halves. These coins, or keys... Time Triggers at any rate... well, they're whole! Michelangelo della wotsit said we needed *one* time trigger to save his sister, not two."

"Come to think of it, so did our lovely Roman friend just now," said Robert. "He said he wanted *one* key... single... not pleural."

Alice looked down at her coin-key thing.

"One time traveller can travel alone with one Trigger... one whole Time Trigger. We just happen to have found two this time," she said.

"Or three?" said Robert.

Alice looked at him. Then, in a flash, she remembered the little pouch. She carefully extracted it from her trouser pocket and palpated the contents through the soft leather. She shot a smile at Robert. Whatever was inside was round like the other two Time Triggers. She loosened the drawstring and gently tipped it out.

Robert whistled. This coin was slightly bigger than the other two and cleaner. It had similar mysterious marks engraved on its bronze surface. Alice felt a flutter of warmth and power shooting through her body.

"It's very beautiful," she whispered.

"Our Roman friend back there was really miffed that we took it," said Robert. "He wants one of these coins or keys or whatever they are, very badly."

"Umm. I noticed," said Alice. "We didn't see any prisoner sisters to rescue though, did we?"

Robert shrugged.

"I'm still wondering why that Michelangelo and Vittoria left their Time Trigger in the mosaic for us to find?" he said. "Why not use it?"

"There must be a reason. It's a part of the quest we haven't worked out yet," said Alice. She was deep in thought. "That Roman boy said we had come to rescue the Briton slave girl. Assuming he was talking about the sister of the guy in the catacombs, does that mean that Michelangelo-wotsit was once a slave too?"

"Seems a bit unlikely," said Robert. "But then again, this time travelling business keeps on surprising me! I suppose it is possible. He's certainly a time traveller because he could see us. And now we know he could have time travelled alone. So that still brings us back to why didn't he go back and get his sister?"

"Oh, dear. We have got some serious thinking to

do," said Alice, putting the third coin carefully away and getting to her feet. "Who *was* that Roman boy? We need to find out which Roman emperor had a withered hand because the dead Roman Caesar did, and he was the boy's father."

Robert nodded.

"Hey!" he said suddenly. "Remember that cyber café we passed near the hotel?"

"Yeah..."

"Well, if we could go on the Internet, we could find out a bit more, maybe."

Alice nodded at Robert. His blue eyes danced with excitement.

Someone was shouting at them. It was Jessica.

"Come on you two!" she called. "Your mum wants to go back to the hotel, Robert."

Robert waved across to his parents.

"Yeah. I'm really starving," said Robert. "What about you, Jess?"

Jessica smiled suspiciously at her cousin, who was in a very good mood all of a sudden.

"Me too. I'm fed up with all these old ruins," she said.

Back at the hotel, Alice wriggled into her one dress and swapped her trainer boots for sandals, smiling to herself as she put the boots carefully in the bottom of her wardrobe. "Thank you," she whispered.

"Come on, then!" she called to Jessica, who was putting the finishing touches to her make-up. "You're beautiful enough. Let's go. The others will be down already I should think."

The two girls descended the marble staircase to the hotel lobby. Robert greeted Alice with a flick of something cold.

"Oy!" said Alice, crossly.

"It's only water," he said, with a dangerous grin.

Using his finger, he was stirring the water in a stone pedestal under a statue of a cherub.

Alice was just about to return the assault when Robert's dad shouted.

"Later…" she hissed menacingly under her breath.

Robert's parents led them through the lamp-lit streets of the metropolis to a cosy restaurant that nestled under the arches next to the famous Spanish Steps.

"*Buona sera*," said a young waiter. He showed them to their table. Alice couldn't help thinking that he would have looked equally at home wearing the helmet, marching boots and overlapping breastplates of the Roman legionaries.

At the medley of pretty tables, Roman families and tourists relaxed together. Candles burned in empty wine bottles. Wax dripped down the bottle necks like molten lava, setting as it cooled into red fronds. The restaurant buzzed with the music of voices and clinking glass.

Alice tried to choose between a pizza or something more adventurous, confused by the delicate smells wafting from other tables.

In the end, the pizza won.

"I bet I'm going to wish I had what you're having when it comes," she said to Robert. "I always do that."

But she was wrong. It was the most delicious pizza she had ever tasted. The edges were crunchy but the middle was lovely and gooey with lots of cheese and not too much tomato. There was a faint, mysterious, herby flavour that was new but very, very nice.

"Want to swap some *pollo al forno?*" offered Robert.

"Looks great chicken… but no thanks," said Alice. The pizza was just too good.

10

The Internet Café

"Italians don't make much of breakfast, do they," said Alice, surveying the meagre offerings the next morning. "I'm surprised. They seem to take lunch and dinner very seriously."

"Don't complain, Alice," said Mrs Davenport. "You'll be back to your bacon and eggs the day after tomorrow."

"Don't like bacon and eggs," muttered Alice.

"Mum," said Robert.

"Yes."

"Can Alice and I go for a walk while you're finishing your breakfast... just to the corner of the street?"

Mrs Davenport nodded curtly, looking pleased to be free of interruptions.

"Can I come?" said Jessica eagerly.

"No," said Robert, standing up next to Alice.

"Come on now, Rob," said Mr Davenport.

"But..."

"You can't leave your cousin out," said Mrs Davenport.

Robert and Alice looked at one another. Alice shrugged. They would just have to distract her somehow.

They walked out of the hotel and stood on the step.

"Look Jessica," said Robert. "Alice and I want to go on the Internet."

"How?" said Jessica.

"In that cyber café," said Alice, pointing.

"*Your* mum won't let you," said Jessica meanly.

"*My* mum won't know."

Robert glared at his cousin.

"I won't tell... if you let me come too," said Jessica.

Robert scowled.

"We haven't got much choice have we? But not on our terminal," said Robert. "You'll have to have your own."

Jessica nodded triumphantly.

It wasn't easy to communicate in the café, but Alice managed to find the right gestures and a weird mixture of English, Italian and even French to get them two PCs and some more breakfast.

Jessica was soon absorbed in a search for English *Harry Potter* sites, while the other two looked for something about Roman Emperors. It didn't take them long to find what they were looking for.

"Stop! Go back," said Alice. "I saw it... look... there! Claudius. He was a cripple."

They read on in silence, scrolling down the pages of Roman history.

"Sounds like a bit of a wimp," said Robert after a few minutes.

"It sounds like him, though, doesn't it?" said Alice. "He took over from his nephew who was assassinated."

"Lots of stabbing and poisoning going on," said Robert.

Alice carried on reading.

"Claudius had one son called Britannicus, named after Claudius' successful invasion of Britain. That's interesting... Claudius was once in Britain." Alice was thoughtful for a moment. "Anyway," she continued. "... then he married Agrippina, after his first wife was conveniently murdered, and he

61

adopted her son, Nero."

"Cool!"

"Hold it," said Alice. "They're the names the Roman boy said, I think."

"Yes, you're right. Agrippina and Nero. He said they killed Claudius. Look... it says the Empress Agrippina did kill Claudius... with poisoned mushrooms. I saw mushrooms on the table," said Robert. "Hey... I bet the boy who chased us was Britannicus, his real son. It says here that he was thirteen when his father was murdered. But he didn't become emperor. Nero, his sixteen-year-old stepbrother did. Agrippina is thought to have murdered Britannicus. She sounds like a really wicked stepmother!"

"And I saw someone else sneaking away through the Roman bath ... I saw a reflection," said Alice.

"Bet it was Nero. He's the one who let Rome burn isn't he?" said Robert.

"Mmm. Nasty piece of work, by the sound of it," said Alice.

"Wow! We were *really* there when Claudius was killed, Alice!" Robert was grinning in delight.

Alice cringed.

"Maybe we went back a bit too late," said Alice. "I think the Roman boy did know why we were there, but we should have gone back before Claudius was murdered."

"But we don't know who we are trying to rescue," said Robert.

"We used the Time triggers just because we fancied going back to Ancient Rome, didn't we?" said Alice. "Not specifically to do with the quest. What we should have done is go back again to Renaissance Rome and talk to the guy in the catacombs and Vittoria. We were a bit hasty, I think.

Time travellers have to respect the power of Time Triggers. We are led to them because we have a job to do. Remember, we have a gift to feel time as it truly is. It is our destiny to harness this power to bring about changes and put right the wrongs of others. I don't think we should just mess about with them whenever we fancy it. We shouldn't have just gone back like that until we knew a bit more. I reckon we were lucky to escape."

"You could be right," said Robert.

"They are powerful things, these Triggers," said Alice.

"Hey!" said Robert. "I think you were right earlier."

"What about?" said Alice.

"I think that freaky earthquake did jumble up the souvenirs at Lincoln Castle so I could find the Time Trigger when I did."

"Yes," said Alice. "And I think it was no accident that my trainer got stuck under the table in the Caesar's palace."

Robert nodded and glanced at his watch.

"Hey, we've been here for a while," he said.

"We must try and time travel back to that Michelangelo guy and Vittoria very soon," whispered Alice, closing down the web site.

"Come on, Jessica," said Robert. "Oooh! Nice piccies."

"I don't fancy him or anything!" said Jessica, snatching up her print outs of a movie star.

"Huh! Not much!" said Robert.

"Let's have a look then," said Alice joining them.

But Jessica folded up her photographs and put them in her pocket.

"Come on. Got to go!" said Robert.

11

Il Colosseo

Mr Davenport was waiting for them on the steps of the hotel.

"Robert! Being late like this is getting beyond a joke!"

"But, it wasn't just me... " said Robert.

"Your mother has gone off in a huff to the shops again!" said Mr Davenport.

"Can't the rest of us go to the Colosseum?" said Alice.

"Hmm. Well... I suppose we could ... "

"Go on, Dad. Mum doesn't really want to go anyway."

"You could leave a message at reception," suggested Alice.

"Yes. I could, I suppose. Good idea, young lady," said Mr Davenport.

"I need the toilet," said Jessica.

"There's one just inside," said Alice.

"Come on then, dear," said Mr Davenport to his niece. "You two wait here."

"I've been thinking," said Robert. "We don't have to sneak off now to St. Peter's or the catacombs to find Vittoria. We could time travel from where we are now and walk back to the Vatican once we're there, in the Sixteenth Century, if you see what I mean?"

"Yes. I think you're right. We should... "

Mr Davenport reappeared through the sliding doors of the hotel with Jessica and put on a baseball cap.

"O.K. gang. Let's go! Onward to the Colosseum!" he said.

Alice and Robert frowned at each other, and followed him. They would just have to wait for now. Alice consoled herself with the chance to go to the real Colosseum that up to now, she had only seen in films and books.

The majestic structure loomed ever closer as they strolled along the Via dei Fori Imperiali. The vast height of this mighty amphitheatre dwarfed the trees and lamp-posts. Alice was silent. It was an archeological beast.

"Did you know that the Colosseum has eighty entrance gates and in it's hey day, it could hold *fifty thousand* spectators!" said Mr Davenport, reading from his guidebook while they queued up to go in.

"Is that bigger than the Millennium Dome?" said Jessica.

"I don't know about that, dear," said her uncle.

"It's flippin' massive!" said Robert, craning his neck to study the four tiers of two thousand-year-old arches towering above them.

Jessica was examining a mini Colosseum on one of the souvenir stalls.

"You American? American dollars?" said the salesman.

Frightened by the eager advances of the vendor, Jessica put the trinket back. The man picked it up and offered it to her again.

"Very good! Very che-e-ep!" said the man. Alice thought he looked like a predator sensing a vulnerable prey.

Jessica retreated to her uncle's shadow in the queue, and tried to look away. The souvenir seller was still calling after her.

"America... very nice! Dollars? I sell che-e-eper!"

But he was soon distracted by another group of tourists.

"Those models are bad copies," said Jessica, looking relieved that he had lost interest in her.

"Why do you say that?" said Robert.

"They're not round," said Jessica.

"Neither is the Colosseum," said Robert. "It's oval, but not a lot of people know that. Look ... "

He borrowed his father's guidebook and showed her an aerial photograph. "See? You'll see better when we get inside."

"Hope that's soon. It's really hot out here," said Alice, putting on her sunglasses. "Please can we get a drink, Mr Davenport?"

Robert's father gave them some euros and they each bought a can of drink from one of the refreshment barrows.

At last they reached the front of the queue.

It was cool in the shade under the ancient masonry. The inside of the greatest stadium ever built was even better than Alice had dreamed. As they climbed higher and higher to the uppermost levels, she began to appreciate its vastness. From up there, they got the same view of the arena as the women and less senior Roman citizens would have had. Alice could almost hear the roar of the five thousand animals that were once slaughtered in a single day and the screams of a hundred thousand defenceless slaves and Christians who met a bloody end amid the cheers of their bloodthirsty spectators. She started to feel sick.

Suddenly she knew she had to get out of this place.

"I feel terrible ... I'll see you outside," she said, running back into the shade of the exit stairway.

"I'll go with her," said Robert hurriedly.

"We'll meet you by the entrance in fifteen minutes," called Mr Davenport.

Alice didn't stop running until she was back through the gates and on to the pavement outside.

"You look very pale. Did you see a ghost?" joked Robert.

"Felt them, more like," panted Alice. "Horrible place!"

"But you, Alice Hemstock... the great archeologist... you were so keen to see it."

"I know. I was. It *is* fantastic. It's just that... well... it *felt* so horrible. I tell you what... I definitely DO NOT want to travel back in time to when this was in use. No way!"

Robert shrugged.

"Let's go and have a look at that big arch, then," he said. "I like the look of all those battle carvings."

Crossing the road to the Arch of Constantine was a bit on the scary side. Fleets of scooters and roaring traffic five lanes wide screamed irreverently around the Colosseum like racing cars on a Grand Prix circuit.

"Now!" yelled Robert, seeing a chance.

They made it to the grassy island and sat down. Alice lay back and let the hot sun bathe her face.

"Need the shades again," said Robert, pulling his sunglasses from his pocket. He rattled his key ring deliberately.

"Oh, no. I'm not keen on this... not time travelling... not here," said Alice, squinting up at Robert.

"We don't have to go back *that* far," he said, gesturing towards the Colosseum. "Like we've done before, if we concentrate on the time when we met Vittoria and that Michelangelo, we should end up there, shouldn't we?"

Alice sat up.

"In theory, yes. I suppose so. But... "

"But nothing! It's now or never. We're going back

to England tomorrow. When are we going to get a better chance?"

Alice considered for a moment.

"Yes. O.K… O.K," she said eventually, and she reached into her own pocket. She withdrew her clenched hand and slowly opened her fingers. The bronze coin from the mosaic in the dome of St. Peter's glinted in the intense sunlight.

"Should I use this one again and leave the other in its pouch?" she said.

"Yeah. It worked fine last time," said Robert.

Looking at each other in silence, they stood up.

"I think we should still hold onto each other when we travel, don't you?" said Alice.

Robert gave Alice a quizzical look.

"Don't get any funny ideas, Robert Davenport!" said Alice. She hoped she wasn't blushing. "It's just in case we don't both travel or something. I don't want to get separated again."

"How sweet of you," said Robert.

Alice scowled at him.

"Yeah! I know! I know! You're right," said Robert grinning.

He held his arm out. With a slight scoff, Alice held Robert's hand and very pointedly, closed her eyes.

"Concentrate on seeing Vittoria," she said.

12

Caravaggio

𝕬 lice saw a fluorescent rainbow of light through the chink in her eyelids and her body felt as if it was being sucked into a tunnel. She was surfing the waves of time. Her senses drowned in the delicious swirl. She catapulted back to the ground, bruising her knees. She listened, half expecting to hear the cheers of a crowded Colosseum. But all was quiet. In a surge of courage, she opened her eyes.

The first thing she looked for was the Colosseum. She could see its skulking silhouette. But to her relief, she saw that some of the arches of the upper tiers were in ruins, although the decay was not as advanced as when she had last seen it in the Twenty First Century.

"I think we did it," she said.

"Yep," said Robert. "Looks about right, judging by the state of the roads and the horses, and the way those people over there are dressed. Some of these imperial arches and things are dirtier than in our time, though."

"Not restored, I suppose," said Alice. "It looks better without high rise tower blocks in the background though!"

"That's true," said Robert. "O.K. Now what? How are we going to find Vittoria?"

"Erhm. Don't think we need to worry about that."

Alice was staring at two people hurrying towards them. She recognised Vittoria's slim, cloaked figure with the tall frame of Michelangelo Merisi da

Caravaggio beside her, his long coat flapping as he walked.

"Result!" murmured Robert triumphantly.

"Quick! Follow me!" said the young man, grabbing Alice's arm roughly.

"Oh, no!" She shrugged herself free of his grip and stood defiantly in front of him. "Not until you give us some answers. What exactly do you want from us?"

The young man scowled at Alice, his face very close to hers. Robert stepped forward aggressively.

"Not here!" hissed the young man. "I cannot be seen out here. Do you not understand? I have taken a great risk to find you. They will hang me!"

"Who will?" said Alice.

"It doesn't matter to you. It's not important. I have done a few bad things. The guards... bah! It is of no consequence! There are more important matters that we have to sort out."

"Such as?" growled Robert menacingly.

"Not here!" said the man again. "Come this way. To the tavern. It is safe there."

Robert shrugged at Alice and nodded a cautious approval. The young man turned briskly, followed by the swirl of Vittoria's cloak and they led Alice and Robert along cobbled alleyways. The air was soured by the fetid stink of poor sanitation. Sinister figures skulked in doorways and somewhere, a child cried. Alice was surprised at the poverty, which was a far cry from the gilded Renaissance treasures more usually depicted in her history textbooks.

They entered a dimly lit wooden building. Thankfully, it smelt more appealing, with a blazing fire and fumes of ale. They sat down around a corner table.

For the first time, Vittoria pushed back her hood. Alice gasped. Vittoria's beautiful face was deeply scarred down one side by claw marks.

She looked at Alice with a serenity that hinted of mild amusement.

"Aha! She is not so pretty now, is she?" said the young man, seeing the look on Alice's face. "You would like to know what happened... I'm surprised you cannot guess!"

"It looks like... "

"The mark of a lion perhaps?" said the young man. "Would that surprise you, when we found you so close to that arena of death?"

Alice nodded.

"But the Colosseum hasn't been used for hundreds of years, surely?" said Robert.

"Of course," said the man. "And it was not even built until after Nero's death. But he and Claudius and the earlier Caesars had other theatres for their games."

His dark eyes stared intently at Alice and then at Robert. He waited for them to understand.

"You have both been back, haven't you?" said Alice excitedly. "You have time travelled back to those times."

"Oh, yes!" said Caravaggio. "And my poor Vittoria here has seen a gladiator's view of a Roman arena a bit too clearly... Agrippina had her thrown to the lions!"

Alice cringed.

The man looked at Vittoria then put his arm around her shoulders. He kissed her head.

"I think it is time for me to explain," he said.

He poured them each a cup of pungent golden liquor from the jug on the table and took a swig of his own.

"I am not who people think I am."

"Who do they think you are?" said Robert.

"To my friends in this age, I am known as Caravaggio the painter. As far as they are concerned, I was born into the Merisi family, in the village of Caravaggio, and named Michelangelo. Thus I would be called Michelangelo Merisi da Caravaggio. Just call me Caravaggio! When my wealthy patrons favour me and keep me out of the prisons... " he chuckled maliciously to himself. "... why then, I paint. I think I even paint quite well, though perhaps my technique is a bit unconventional for most people's taste in this age, where the painter should do as he is told and paint what he is asked by his employers. Not me! Oh, sometimes I must be a good boy, just to get paid and to eat. But I prefer to paint as I see, not as I am told to do. Is that not so, Vittoria?"

Vittoria smiled.

"My beautiful Vittoria knows! May I present to you the granddaughter of the *other* Michelangelo!"

"You are Michelangelo's granddaughter? Wow!" said Alice.

The young woman nodded.

"Oh, yes, my friends!" continued Caravaggio, with an edge of mockery in his voice. "The great Michelangelo!"

"But he *was* great," said Alice. "He designed the dome of St. Peter's, and made all those wonderful marble sculptures and painted the Sistine Chapel and... "

"Oh, yes indeed. One of the greatest artists that will ever walk the earth, that is sure," said Caravaggio. "But he never recognised Vittoria's mother as his child. It was not permitted. Vittoria's grandmother was a Marchioness no less." He laughed cruelly. "Vittoria is an artist too. She earns a little money by working on the mosaic in St. Peter's and she helps me with many of my paintings."

"Haven't you thought of time travelling back to see your grandfather, Vittoria?" said Alice. "Wouldn't it be amazing to sit beside him on his scaffolding as he painted away on one of his frescoes! I would love to meet him face to face."

"How do you know that she has not?" said Caravaggio mischievously. Alice's eyes widened.

"Are you two... well... *together?*" asked Robert, rather bashfully.

"Are we lovers, do you mean?"

Caravaggio looked at Vittoria and shook his head from side to side, playfully pretending not to know.

"But you are both time travellers, aren't you?" said Alice.

"Indeed we are... well... were."

"*Were?*" said Robert.

"I got greedy, didn't I? I did the unmentionable."

Robert and Alice looked at each other in confusion.

"I travelled *forwards* as well as back, didn't I? And lost my power."

"You used a Time Trigger and travelled into the future?" said Robert, wide-eyed in excitement.

"Oh, yes! Just for the fun of it! I got away with it several times. I went further forward than this. Why do you think the style of my art is so revolutionary for these times? I have read in the art books of the future that my work is the toast of the art world in the Twentieth Century. I am to be 're-discovered'!"

He raised his cup in a mock toast to his own greatness. "Lucky me! They will call me the Master of Darkness. Go and look for yourself, when you return to your own time. Look closely at my work that is supposed to inspire so many of your great artists of tomorrow. Do you know... can you imagine... what it is like to look at my own paintings that I have yet to paint?"

"Cool," said Robert.

"Cool? What is this *cool*? Why do you not say *hot*?" said Caravaggio.

"Well, you *could*... " began Robert. Caravaggio interrupted him by waiving his arm dismissively.

"There are more important issues to discuss, my friends," he said.

Alice took a mouthful of her drink. So that was why Caravaggio had not used the Time Trigger to rescue his sister. He couldn't. He had lost his powers by recklessly travelling forwards.

"Wow!" she spluttered, swallowing hard. The ale was strong and intoxicating. Robert tried his. He grinned, before draining the cup. His cheeks reddened slightly and his smile faded, as the liquor warmed his stomach a bit too quickly.

"Ooops!" he said.

He hiccuped quietly. It was more like a squeak. Alice frowned at him.

"I hope you're not going to get drunk. We need to concentrate," she said.

"I'm cool," said Robert, trying to look serious.

Caravaggio clucked at the interruption.

"You two *children,* it would seem, are our only hope of getting Octavia back," he said.

"Octavia?" said Robert. "That's a new one!"

"Octavia is my sister," said Caravaggio. "That is no more her birth name than the name I now use. But like chameleons, we have changed our names in order to survive. She is still back in Ancient Rome, trapped by Agrippina and her hateful sons." He spat on the floor. "It is up to you now to get her out."

13

The Keys of Rome

Alice shuddered at the thought of going back to Ancient Rome.

"There is more, my friends. If you do not succeed, the face of Britain as you know it could change in the flash of a Time Crash. The civilization that has flourished since the Roman occupation under Claudius will crumble to nothing if you do not put the keys back in the Lindum Shield where they belong."

"Woah! Hold on a minute, mate," said Robert. He drew up his stool closer to the table. "I am really getting confused now. Can you give us a little more help here? If your sister is back in Claudian Rome and you're a famous Renaissance painter, buddy-buddy with young Michelwotsit's granddaughter here, well... how can that be? How is this Octavia your sister? I'm sorry, but I just can't work it out!"

Robert was definitely slurring his speech a little, but Alice had to agree with him. It didn't make any sense.

"And what is a Time Crash?" said Alice.

Caravaggio grinned at them.

"Octavia is my sister because I am also a Briton. I have travelled forward from Ancient Rome where we were taken as slaves."

Robert and Alice looked at each other and nodded.

"I have adopted the name Michelangelo Merisi da Caravaggio. There was a plague in the village of Caravaggio in the year 1576, just before I chanced to arrive here as a boy, escaping from my Roman captors by time travelling. Most of the Merisi family had died. It was easy for me to take the name. I have always been good at painting, even before we were enslaved, so I have survived by developing my skills in this time... what you call the Renaissance, I think."

"You were captured by the Romans when they invaded Britain?" said Alice.

"By the emperor Claudius himself!" said Caravaggio bitterly. "In Briton, I was the son of the leader of the Corieltauvi Tribe."

Deep in Alice's memory she had a flash of something she had seen before. She saw again the misty marshes and the legionaries marching along the straight road to Lincoln.

"Claudius recognised our worth. We were to be used as bait for our father. Octavia and I were betrayed to Claudius. Thankfully, our younger sister Bardecia, escaped. But to my eternal regret... " Caravaggio thumped the table with his fist. "... we unknowingly lead Claudius to the shield... and to... the keys."

"O.K. I'm with you so far. Your father was the chieftain of the Corieltauvi Tribe of Ancient Britons and you and one of your sisters were captured by Claudius when he invaded. Now might be a good time to tell us about this *shield*?" said Robert.

Caravaggio took another gulp of ale.

"The Lindum Shield... that's what it was named by Claudius, and what it will come to be known as, by the archaeologists of your time... if you succeed, that is, in your task to restore the Time Triggers. It was the source of power for the holy men and women of our tribe for countless generations. It is a rectangular plaque cast in the Iron Age. Its power came from the three ancient pendants set within it. When they are all in place, like keys, they unlock the healing and magical powers of the shield for the elders of our tribe to use for the good of our people. Claudius dumped the shield and took the pendants. They are not coins... they are the Corieltauvi Keys. I think they would now be better called The Keys of Rome."

Alice put her hand on the table. She slowly unfurled her fingers and lifted her hand away, revealing her round piece of mosaic. Vittoria drew in her breath. Caravaggio turned to look at Robert expectantly. With a droopy grin, Robert unclipped the key ring from his belt and put his own talisman on the table. He looked at Alice expectantly. But Alice decided not to reveal the third key just yet. She still didn't fully trust Caravaggio. Robert raised one eyebrow but said nothing. Everyone looked at the keys.

"They don't look like much, do they?" said Robert.

"But you know their power," said Caravaggio. "Where did you find the second one?"

"I bought it from the shop at Lincoln Castle."

"Back in Britain?" said Caravaggio.

Robert nodded.

"Then Claudius must have lost it before he came back to Rome," said Caravaggio. "There was a third. I have a feeling Claudius hid it somewhere. It is my hope that Octavia will know where. If not, you may have to search for it."

Robert looked across at Alice and winked. She smiled slightly.

"Was Claudius a time traveller then?" said Robert.

"Yes. That was unfortunately one of his many talents... as well as murder and theft. He used his powers to advance himself as ruler of an empire. He was a clever man, as many evil leaders are. He only found out that he was a time traveller by accident though, when he got his snidey little paws on the shield. My father gave the shield, and his life, to protect my sisters and me, and the future of our people. But that crippled coward sent me and Octavia back to Rome as slaves anyway."

"But you escaped?" said Alice.

Caravaggio nodded.

"Yes. Octavia caught the fancy of Agrippina, Claudius' wife. I think she thought there was something exotic about the daughter of a tribal chieftain. It certainly boosted Claudius' popularity with the citizens of Rome. She was made a Vestal Virgin."

"Was that some kind of punishment?" said Alice.

"Not to Roman women. Only women of noble birth are usually admitted as priestesses to the sect of Vesta. Probably a relief to most of them ... escaping the clutches of the senators and generals. Octavia is of noble birth. I think she was a kind of trophy for Claudius."

"Was Agrippina a time traveller?" asked Alice.

"Yes. But not her spawn, Nero!" Caravaggio spat on the ground. "And Claudius' son, Britannicus, was. Agrippina would stop at nothing to protect Nero's interests. She wanted her own son to succeed Claudius as Caesar. She knew about the power of the keys and how Britannicus could use one of them to threaten Nero. She was desperate to find the keys and keep them from Britannicus. I pity Britannicus' chances of staying alive after his father's death without a key!"

"So how did *you* escape then?" said Robert.

"Octavia got a key back from Claudius. She stole it from him. She threw it to me during one of the races and it saved my life."

"Races?" said Robert.

"Chariot races. I was a slave charioteer."

Robert whistled.

"It was that or be sacrificed as a gladiator. But Claudius respected my skills with a horse. To Claudius, nothing mattered more than the violence and sport of the races. I think he would have loved to see me die there. But I disappointed him!" Caravaggio smiled triumphantly.

"So why didn't you go back for your sister?" said Alice.

Caravaggio fell silent. Remorse filled his face. His eyes misted with sadness.

"Because I was a fool," he said.

Nobody dared speak for a few minutes. Robert broke the silence.

"Like an idiot, you couldn't resist playing with the Time Trigger for a while could you? Tut, tut!"

Caravaggio glared straight at Robert. The two young men looked strangely alike in the flickering half-light.

"Could you honestly tell me that you would not ever be tempted?" said Caravaggio.

14

The Quest Unveiled

Alice stood up.

"I need some fresh air," she said. The others looked at her. "It's O.K! I don't think I'm about to time travel ... it's just the wine, I think."

Robert smiled rather stupidly and swigged the last of his drink. Alice was feeling a bit sick, but this nausea was different from the time travelling type, which was almost like having butterflies in your tummy. This time, she felt dangerously close to actually being sick.

"Please can we go for a walk ... outside?" she asked.

Caravaggio shrugged and gestured reluctantly towards the door. Robert dragged himself up, rubbing his head.

"Mmm. Might need a couple of Mum's headache tablets when we get back," he muttered sorrowfully.

They left the inn and walked out into the streets of Sixteenth Century Rome. Alice soon felt much better. She was deep in thought, trying to fit the pieces of the jigsaw together in her head. It was clear that Caravaggio was a time traveller refugee, marooned here in Renaissance Rome by his own misadventures in the future. What were she and Robert supposed to do next? Presumably, Octavia was a time traveller too. But even if they used the coins ... or keys ... to go back to the Claudian era, how would they find her? And if travelling into the future had affected Caravaggio, would it be safe to try to bring her forwards in time to escape?

Alice was getting a headache now. She looked back at Robert. He was looking very grey and sorry for himself.

"We're going back home to England tomorrow evening," she said eventually. "That doesn't leave us much time to save Octavia *and* the future of Britain from a Time Crash thing-a-me-gig! We don't even know where the Lindum Shield is now."

They entered a bustling market square. Alice whistled at the unexpected riot of colour. Swathes of chilli peppers tumbled down the sides of vegetable stalls into crates of lemons.

They mingled with merchants, servants and papal dignitaries amongst the stalls of traders offering fish and meat and fruit and flowers.

"Umm. That's different," said Robert as they emerged into a central clearing.

"A gallows!" said Alice, shuddering.

Caravaggio nodded. He mockingly blew a kiss at the ominous structure.

Alice looked at Vittoria. She was beckoning to them from across the square. She pointed at some-one. They followed her gaze.

Two official looking guards on chestnut horses were riding slowly through the throng in their direction. The horses' tails swished at flies.

"Uh, oh!" hissed Caravaggio. "Come on! This way."

They ducked between the crowds and Alice bumped into a fat merchant.

"Oh, sorry..." she said automatically. She shook her arm to get rid of the electric feeling generated by the contact.

The man was surprised by the jolt. He looked around for the culprit and starting shouting abuse at a nearby stallholder.

"He can't see you," said Robert, grinning.

"Where's Vittoria gone?" said Alice.

"Over there," said Robert, pointing. "Just a sec..."

Robert pinched the fat man's bottom and jumped away, skillfully avoiding the man's clench fist as he turned to confront his invisible assailant.

"This brings a whole new dimension to 'tig'!" spluttered Robert in between giggles.

"No time!" said Alice.

Vittoria's cloaked silhouette vanished down an alleyway. She disappeared through an arched door into a gloomy interior.

"More creepy places," said Robert. "Why are you always hiding in sewers and catacombs, Caravaggio? Do you like the villainous company in these places?"

For a second time, the two young men glared at one another. Caravaggio's cat-like body tensed and his curled lips twitched.

"O.K. guys," said Alice. "We have a quest, remember? Octavia? Claudius? Keys? Shields?"

Carravagio relaxed and backed away a few paces. He spat on to the floor, still looking at Robert. His eyes danced with a mixture of amusement and hatred.

"Let's talk," he said, leaning against the wall.

Vittoria poked the meagre fire, sending sparks up the chimney. A rat scurried from behind the woodpile.

"Urggh! Can we get on with it, please," said Alice.

She shuddered. It was cold in the hovel and there was nowhere to sit. Robert perched on the edge of an old table.

"What's the plan then?" he said casually.

Carravaggio looked at Vittoria and took a deep breath.

"You have to go back and get Octavia. I can't."

Robert was about to say something provocative,

but Alice glared at him.

"Right," said Robert eventually. "O.K. So what happens if we... can't find her?"

"If Claudius dies, she will die," said Caravaggio.

"Why?" said Alice.

"Because Agrippina and Britannicus are both using Octavia as bait to trap me. They know I have the key. Britannicus wants a key very badly... with it he could outwit Agrippina and her plans for Nero to succeed Claudius. Agrippina knows this and she wants to get to the key first. But if she manages to kill Claudius, Nero will succeed him anyway and Agrippina will have no more need of Octavia, so she will have her killed."

Alice and Robert nodded gravely. Caravaggio continued.

"You MUST go back for her, find the third key and then... take the keys back to Britain. They must be returned to our younger sister, Bardecia. I am sure she will know the whereabouts of the Lindum Shield. This must happen for history to follow the path that you and I have seen, both here and in Britain."

"Otherwise this Time Crash thing-a-me-gig?" said Robert.

"Yes!" said Caravaggio.

"We have to rescue Octavia from the delightful Agrippina and Britannicus. Then we smuggle the keys back to England and... what then? Time travel there and give them back to your other sister?" said Robert.

"Yes! At last!" Caravaggio glared mockingly at Alice and Robert. "Finally you understand what you must do."

"You have *got* to be joking!" said Robert.

"Joking? Why would I joke?"

"You seriously expect us to snatch your sister from

under the watchful eyes of those treacherous Romans?" said Robert.

"Well *I* can't!"

"That's not *our* fault!" said Robert. "Or *our* responsibility."

"Oh, yes it is, my friend. Why else would you have found the keys? It is up to you two now."

"Why can't *she* try?" said Robert, pointing unkindly at Vittoria. He was beginning to look a little pale and very serious now.

"Don't you think she has tried?" said Caravaggio.

"Is that when Vittoria got the claw marks?" said Alice.

Caravaggio nodded. Vittoria withdrew further beneath the hood of her cloak.

"It's O.K.," said Alice reassuringly.

"Agrippina," murmured Vittoria, shaking slightly.

"It was the last time I was able to use my key," said Caravaggio. "Thankfully I got Vittoria out just in time. I have tried to use the key since, but all I get is pain when I touch it now. I must have used it recklessly to go forward too many times. And Vittoria is too afraid to try alone. So we stuck it to the dome of St. Peter's Cathedral. It felt right there. As if... somehow... more of the chosen ones who have the power to time travel might find it and travel back to us. We were right, my love." He glanced at Vittoria. "These two are the ones. But... they are not strong enough!"

Robert jumped off the table with a sudden forcefulness.

"Aren't we?" he said.

Alice looked at him in surprise.

"Do you really think we can do it?" she said.

"Well, if we don't go back," said Robert. "our homes might not exist. Lincoln and Newark might

84

not exist. Maybe *we* won't even exist! We'll all go pop in a Time Crash! Yum, yum!"

Caravaggio looked doubtfully at Robert.

"Even if you do go back, there is one big problem that may yet undo us all," he said gravely. "The third key. It is the central pendant. It is very like the other two but slightly larger. If you cannot find it, then your quest will be in vain."

"Uh, huh," said Alice, smiling.

Caravaggio frowned at her. She reached into the depths of one of her pockets and brought out the pouch.

"This key?" she said, sliding the Time Trigger into her palm.

15

The Chariot Race

C aravaggio's eyes widened in surprise. He looked at
Alice. A smile crept across his sunburnt features
and his eyes shone with admiration.

"I see that you, too, have secrets," he said. "Where
did you get this one?"

"From Claudius, I suspect," said Alice. "He left us
a little present hidden under a table."

"Does this mean that you have already had the
pleasure of meeting that despot?" said Caravaggio.

"Um... not exactly," said Robert. "Claudius was a
dead body when we got there. But Alice found the
third key. It's a long story involving shoelaces and
tables!"

"Spare me the details!" said Caravaggio, chuckling. "You two are worthy travellers after all. So...
Claudius is dead. Time is running out for
Britannicus then. And for Octavia. You must go
back for her soon, my friends. And then... you can
return ALL the keys to their rightful place in the
shield."

"So how do we find Octavia then?" said Robert.

"Vittoria will show you. Although she was too
afraid to return alone, after what happened last time,
she has asked to accompany you two. She has never
lost her powers. I'm the only one who played with the
forces of time and tried to outwit them," said
Caravaggio.

"Do you think we should go back now?" said Alice.
Caravaggio nodded.

"But we've never done that before... travelled

further back from already *being* back… if you see what I mean?" said Robert.

"It should be O.K," said Alice. "We're still going backwards from the Twenty First Century."

"As long as we don't try and go further into the future than our own time, we'll be O.K?" asked Robert.

Caravaggio nodded.

Alice put the third Time Trigger safely in her pocket and offered Vittoria her hand. In the other hand, she clutched her other key. Robert linked arms with her. Alice thought she saw him give Caravaggio a provocative wink just before closing his eyes.

"Just a minute!" shouted Caravaggio. "Take this. You might need it."

He thrust a dagger into Vittoria's hand. Before anyone had time to protest, the three of them were spinning once again, through the chaos of time. Alice felt sicker than ever. She heard Vittoria yelling something in Italian. It sounded like trouble and with butterflies dancing in her stomach, she opened her eyes.

"Oh, no!" screamed Alice.

Unfortunately, they had travelled back right into the middle of a chariot race.

"The Circus Maximus!" cried Robert.

"Move, you idiot!" shouted Alice.

They all flung themselves against the perimeter wall to avoid the lethal wheels and hooves.

"Come on!" said Robert, leaping over the wall into the seating behind. The front rows of seats were sculpted in marble. Robert, Alice and Vittoria settled themselves into some empty places. The seating behind was wooden. Alice thought this would be for the less important citizens. Beyond that, was standing room only. All the men wore togas. Everyone was yelling and shouting passionately. There seemed to be four teams, with drivers wearing green, blue, red or white.

"It's just like watching *Forest*," said Alice, remembering the last time she had accompanied her father and Granddad to a football match in Nottingham.

"Wicked!" said Robert. "I wish we could have a go."

There were ten chariots being furiously driven around the track, pulled by two, three or four horses. Dust flew as they jostled and scraped. The noise from the crowd was deafening. As the two leaders rounded the bend in front of them, each furiously whipping their horses, the nearest chariot started to tip outwards, like a windsurfer out of control.

"Oh, no! It's going to overturn!" yelled Alice.

Just as the chariot was about to hit the ground, the driver pulled out a knife and cut himself free from the reins that were tied around his waist. He fell from the chariot on to the sand and rolled to safety. The crowd roared as the other chariot took over the lead.

Alice coughed in the dust. As the cloud settled, she glanced aside. Only a few metres away, someone was watching them. One spectator at least could see them. She pulled Robert's sleeve.

"We've got company," she said.

Vittoria slowly stood up. Alice saw her hiding Caravaggio's dagger under her cloak.

"Trouble!" said Robert.

"Britannicus!" breathed Alice.

The young man was staring at them.

"I think this is the first time he's ever seen us," whispered Alice.

"And he *can* definitely see us," said Robert.

"What do you suggest we do?" said Alice.

"He's not expecting *us*, is he?" said Robert.

"No. He's been waiting for Caravaggio. He won't know who we are."

"Let's introduce ourselves then... he might lead us to Octavia," said Robert.

"Hang on... "

But Robert was already walking towards the other boy, holding out his hand. For a moment, Britannicus hesitated. There were a group of soldiers only metres behind him. But he did not alert them to the children's presence. He was looking at their clothes, especially at Alice. She tried to smile at him. An older boy behind Britannicus shouted angrily at one of the teams, punching the air aggressively. Britannicus followed her gaze.

"Nero?" said Alice.

Vittoria shrank behind Robert and Alice.

Britannicus nodded slowly. A shadow of fear crossed his handsome face.

"You brother can't see us, can he?" said Alice.

Britannicus shook his head, smirking slightly.

"*Pax vobiscum!*" he said finally. "Welcome! You have come for Octavia?"

"How is it that you speak our language as well as Latin?" asked Alice.

"I have travelled to a later time with my father's key. That was before the slave's brother disappeared with it," said Britannicus.

"Your father's key?" said Robert.

"Yes," said Britannicus.

"Your father stole it. It belongs to a British tribe," said Robert.

"The Britons are slaves," said Britannicus. "Slaves cannot own anything."

"They are people, like me and you," said Alice with

a sudden burst of anger.

"Ha! Slaves are slaves. They are the property of their owner. That is the law."

"Then not all laws are... well... right. Bad laws should be changed," said Alice.

Britannicus looked at her for a moment. There was respect in his dangerous eyes.

"Oh, don't waste your breath, Alice," said Robert. "Let's keep our mind on our job here, shall we?"

Alice glared defiantly at the young Roman..

"You said you used the key to go *forward?*" asked Robert.

Britannicus gave Alice a last lingering stare before turning to Robert.

"Yes. Several times," he replied.

Alice and Robert looked at one another.

"Did it hurt to hold the key the last time you touched it?" said Alice.

"Yes, it did. How did you know?"

"He doesn't know he can't use it again!" whispered Robert.

Alice gave Robert a little nod. She looked at Vittoria, who raised one eyebrow, as if she too understood what Britannicus did not.

"May I... have a look at your key?" asked Britannicus, edging closer to Alice.

"No!" said Robert. He stepped between Alice and Britannicus. "First you will have to take us to Octavia. Then you can have a key."

"Are you offering him a deal?" whispered Alice incredulously.

"Uh, huh," said Robert. "Inspired, wouldn't you say. He can't pick the keys up anyway."

Alice grinned. Robert was right. It was a brilliant idea.

"You'll give me a key in exchange for Octavia?"

said Britannicus.

"Absolutely!" said Robert.

"What will you do with a key?" asked Alice.

"Escape from my stepmother," said Britannicus. "She plans to kill my father, the Emperor Claudius. Then she will kill me, so that her own son, Nero . . . " he pointed over his shoulder. " . . . so *he* can be Caesar."

"Sounds like a stepmother from hell!" said Robert.

"So your father isn't dead yet?" said Alice.

Britannicus looked puzzled. He shook his head slowly.

"Then we haven't met before at all?" said Alice.

Again, Britannicus shook his head.

"You were right," whispered Robert. "When we met this guy yesterday, it was in his future. That's why he recognised us. But now we've travelled back to before Claudius was murdered."

Britannicus looked between the three visitors for a moment. Then he turned impatiently.

16

ℬetrayed

𝕋 hey followed Britannicus along the Roman streets.

"Keep your wits about you!" whispered Robert. "This could be a trap."

They were soon down to the banks of the River Tiber. Barge cargoes were being unloaded in the busy Port of Rome. Spicy fragrance lingered in the air. Pottery jars, emptied of their store of olive oil, lay smashed on the quayside.

They turned back down a straight road heading for the Roman Forum. Alice noticed that tall apartment blocks were crammed closely together and washing hung between the balconies. It reminded her in some ways of modern Rome, two thousand years later.

Britannicus stopped to take a drink of water from a street fountain.

"Please... help yourselves. The sun is very hot," he said to the others.

Alice looked longingly at the sparkling liquid.

"Is it safe to drink?" she asked.

"Of course!" laughed Britannicus. "This is Rome! Our clean water is carried into the city from the aqueducts."

"Umm. Built by slaves like those, I suppose?" said Alice, watching some Roman soldiers herding a miserable group of prisoners of war.

Britannicus just shrugged, stepping on to the steps of the fountain to keep clear of a passing funeral procession heading from the Forum towards the burial grounds outside the city walls.

"Go on," said Robert to Alice and Vittoria, when the trumpeters and mourners and black sacrificial pigs had past. He indicated the drinking fountain. "I'll keep watch on our new friend."

The girls took turns to quench their thirsts. And then Robert.

"And is this young beauty for you, my friend?" said Britannicus over his shoulder to Robert, looking at Alice. "And this dark-haired girl too? Pity about the scars, but she might make a good second wife."

Robert choked on the water he was drinking. He stood up, wiping his chin. Alice crossed her arms and tried to stifle a grin, waiting for his reply.

"Er... no... that is... we don't... "

"Women and men are equals in our time, actually," said Alice. "*He's* not mine and we're certainly not *his!*"

"Interesting," said Britannicus, leering at Alice.

He took a step closer to her. Then he glanced up, distracted by a sudden movement over one of the balconies above. He jumped backwards.

An unpleasant smelling collection of household waste splattered on to the cobbles between them.

Britannicus roared with laughter at their surprise.

"Nice of you to warn us, mate!" snapped Robert.

"Yeah. Cheers!" said Alice.

Vittoria wiped some small bones and vegetable skins from the hem of her cloak.

"You shouldn't complain," said Britannicus. "It could have been their toilets."

Alice and Robert grimaced at one another.

"Come on," said Robert. "Let's get going."

With a final snigger, Britannicus turned and lead them past a bustling, organised world of stalls and shops, public baths and building sites. Alice watched as one man carefully weighed fruit into the basket of a balancing device. And she caught a glimpse of a crowd shouting bids for some kind of auction.

"What's going on over there?" she asked Britannicus.

"Slave auction," he said. "Greeks and Britons mostly," he added maliciously.

Alice glanced sadly in their direction.

"I hope you get kind masters," she wished under her breath.

The architecture was getting more elaborate now. The densely packed apartments gave way to formidable arches and Corinthian columns. These were the temples and law courts of the Imperial Roman Forum. Alice noticed that in Claudian Rome, there were fewer buildings than in the maps of Ancient Rome she had seen. Then she realised that more were yet to be built, by later Caesars, like Trajan.

"This way," hissed Britannicus.

He took them up some steps between the mighty columns of a temple porch.

"Wait here. I will bring her out."

Britannicus vanished inside through a heavy door.

"This stinks!" said Robert.

Vittoria was shaking her head.

"Too... how you say it? Too... easy," she said.

Alice nodded emphatically.

"Come on," said Alice. "Round the side. We can watch from there."

They sprang down the steps to the corner of the building and cautiously peered around the edge.

"We should be reasonably safe," said Robert. "Only Britannicus can see us, remember."

"I still don't like it. Keep down," said Alice. "I can't believe he'll just hand over Octavia."

"Sshhh! Someone's coming back out!" said Robert.

The big door opened. They held their breath. To

Alice's surprise, only a young woman stepped out, closing the door behind her. She was dressed in the white robes of a priestess and her face was partly veiled. She peered around her nervously.

"Now what?" said Robert, frowning.

Just then, they heard the sound of marching footsteps rounding the building from the other side. Britannicus was leading the soldiers.

"I thought so," said Alice, shrinking back around the corner.

Robert was just about to say something when Vittoria dashed forward towards the young woman, shouting Octavia's name. She withdrew something from her cloak.

"Uh, oh!" said Robert.

With a glance at Alice, he sprang after Vittoria heroically.

"I really hope these guys can't see me!" he shouted.

Luckily, he was right. The Roman soldiers were frantically rushing around on the steps of the temple like ants, blind to the enemy. Britannicus grabbed the young priestess and held her roughly.

Vittoria walked straight up to Britannicus, with Robert a few steps behind. Alice nimbly wove her way in between the flailing soldiers and caught the other two up.

"Hang on a minute, Vittoria!" shouted Robert.

But she was already threatening the Roman boy with Caravaggio's dagger.

With a sneer across his face, Britannicus drew a knife from his own tunic.

"Give me a key!" he said, holding the sharp blade beside the young woman's throat.

"No!" said Alice.

But to her amazement, Vittoria suddenly stopped and took a step back. She was trying to tell Robert something. The veil had blown from the priestess' face. The frightened young girl was looking straight through them.

"She can't see me," muttered Alice. "Robert!" she called. "This priestess can't see us. It's not her! That's what Vittoria is trying to tell us. This is NOT Octavia!"

17

The Temple of Vesta

Robert understood.

"Now might be a good time to disappear, then!" he called.

He pulled Vittoria backwards and Alice grabbed his other arm.

"Ready?" he shouted.

Alice nodded, gripping her key. She clenched her teeth.

"No!" shouted Britannicus, releasing his frightened hostage and leaping towards them. "Not yet! I need a key!"

"Tough!" said Robert. "Now!" he called across to Alice.

She closed her eyes and from deep inside herself, she concentrated on a power that started to fill her with an intense heat. Just in time, they were travelling in time again, escaping the Roman swords and Britannicus' dagger.

They were back in the Sixteenth Century, sitting in a heap amongst the ruins of the once great Forum.

"Well, that was a waste of time," said Robert. But he was grinning. "Bit of a laugh, though."

"Idiot! We could have been killed if one of those soldiers' swords had hit us," said Alice crossly.

Robert taunted her with pursed lips.

Vittoria stood up. She pointed to the ruined steps and stumps of columns next to them. She started speaking excitedly.

"What are you trying to tell us?" said Alice. "Hang on ... I know ... *Si! Si!* That's it. We didn't waste our time. I think what Vittoria is trying to say is that Britannicus has showed us where the Temple of Vesta is. If we time travel back right here ... well, we might be able to get in and find Octavia ourselves."

"Cool!" said Robert. "Let's do it!"

Vittoria beamed at the other two. She knew they understood. She offered them each an arm.

"I'm gonna need a MASSIVE ice cream and a HUGE drink after this," said Robert. "It's hard work, all this time travelling."

Alice agreed. She was beginning to feel very tired too. But they had to keep going if they were going to rescue Octavia.

"Concentrate on going back then," she said. "But maybe a little bit later on? I don't want to run into Britannicus if I can help it."

"Oh? I thought you two were getting on like a house on fire," said Robert.

Alice glared at him. Then she turned to Vittoria. The other girl nodded and smiled, before closing her green eyes.

Yet again, they time travelled. The nausea was less than last time, but Alice's senses went on overdrive. She gripped Vittoria's arm and breathed deeply. She felt her knees grazing against cold stone and slowly she opened her eyes.

They were surrounded by the darkness of night. The ancient city was quiet now.

"Let's see if we can find a back door," said Robert.

The girls followed him along the alleyway beside the large building.

"Excellent!" said Robert, stopping suddenly a few moments later beside a recessed archway.

He yanked the handle on the single door. But nothing happened.

"Need a hand?" said Alice.

She put her arms around Robert's waist, and felt Vittoria doing the same thing around her. Together they pulled. The door suddenly gave way. Alice heard a little ripping sound as she stood on Vittoria's long dress.

"Oops! Sorry," she said.

Vittoria just smiled and followed Robert through the narrow opening into the lamp-lit interior.

"Looks promising," he said.

They made their way along deserted marble corridors until they came to an elaborate golden shrine sprinkled with flower petals. The chamber smelt with their delicate perfume. The time travellers spread out and started looking around.

"More mosaics," breathed Alice. Finely worked pictures of flowers, goddesses and animals danced across the wall.

"Alice!"

She turned at the sound of her name.

"Wow!" she said, as she saw Vittoria.

The young Italian girl had changed into the robes of a priestess, her face covered by a veil. Vittoria was standing in front of the door to an inner room. Alice could see white clothing hanging inside.

"Cool!" said Robert. "Are you going to sneak in among them and find Octavia? Only joking!"

"Er, I don't think *she* is," said Alice.

Vittoria signalled to them to stay out of sight. Then before they could do anything, she disappeared through another archway into the hallway beyond.

"So what are we supposed to do? Just wait around?" said Robert.

"It's worth a try," said Alice.

"I suppose it has to be Vittoria who looks for Octavia. Neither of us know what she looks like," said Robert.

"Poor Vittoria. She must be very frightened. Don't forget what happened to her last time," said Alice.

Robert made pretend snarling noises, then smiled.

"Yeah. I know. The Romans are a pretty savage lot. Makes you glad to be living when we do, eh?"

Alice nodded.

"Clever, though," said Robert, admiring a collection of bronze statues.

"Can you hear something?" said Alice.

"Yes. Someone's coming. Come on! Get behind this altar thing . . . just in case we can be seen by anyone!"

They ducked behind the decorated shrine just as two women ran in.

"Psst!" said Robert. "Over here."

Vittoria led another young priestess towards them.

"Octavia . . . " she said, smiling at the other girl.

The girl pushed back her veil and Alice saw a resemblance to Caravaggio straight away, although Caravaggio's eyes and hair were darker and his tanned skin now bore testimony to many years under a hot Italian sun. But with her blue eyes and auburn hair, this young woman was not of Roman birth. In fact, Alice thought her complexion was not unlike her own.

Tears were running down the girl's cheeks.

"Hi. I'm Rob," said Robert, holding out his hand and smiling warmly. "I'm very pleased to have found you at last. Relieved actually. Do you think we can get out of here now?"

The girl took his hand and nodded a greeting. Then they heard the sound of more footsteps approaching.

"I think you know what this is," said Alice, showing Octavia her key

The girl nodded.

"Think of your brother," said Alice.

Alice took Robert's hand and linked arms with

Octavia. She kept her eyes open just long enough to see an evil looking woman striding into the room.

"Agrippina!" muttered Vittoria, taking a sharp breath.

It was the same woman Alice had seen leaving the villa where Claudius had been murdered. She closed her eyes and concentrated her thoughts on travelling back to meet Caravaggio to reunite him with his sister. The power of the keys hurled them through an arc of more than five hundred thousand sunsets, condensed and compressed into a few deep breaths.

She opened her eyes sharply, suddenly remembering that for Octavia, this would be travelling forwards in time.

But to her relief, they were back where they wanted to be and Octavia was safely beside her. But then she noticed.

"Oh, no!" she gasped. "Where is Vittoria?"

18

Spots and Paintings

Robert groaned.

"Vittoria has been left behind!" he said. "We're going to have to go back ... *again!*"

Someone was coming towards them, waving. It was Caravaggio.

"How *does* he do it?" said Robert. "He's always in the right place at the right time."

"Dunno. A mysterious man of many talents," said Alice, looking at the young painter.

"Octavia!" he breathed, hugging his sister tightly.

But she pulled away from him. She spoke to her brother in a new dialect that Alice presumed must be the language of the Corieltauvi tribe of Ancient Britain.

Caravaggio turned to them.

"Please ... my Vittoria ... marooned without a Time Tigger, she will not remain invisable!"

"Yeah. Yeah. We've got to go back and get her," said Robert sarcastically. "You really do owe us ... big time!"

Alice felt a sudden wave of nausea coursing through her body.

"Oh. No! Rob! Rob ... do you feel it too?"

Robert nodded. He reached for her hand and before they had a chance to say anything to Caravaggio, they were once more travelling through time, spinning in a vortex of stars and moons back towards their own time.

They were among the grass-covered ruins, not far from their hotel.

"Oops!" said Robert. "If I remember rightly, we were outside the Colosseum last time we were in the Twenty First Century. Let's run back. My dad might get worried if we're not there."

They stood up and ran back down the tree lined Via dei Fori Imperiali, towards the Colosseum. Alice was exhausted. Time travelling sapped her energy even more than a sleep-over.

"I need to crash," she puffed. "I think I'll skip dinner after this."

Mr Davenport and Jessica were walking towards them.

"Oh, there you are! Are you all right now, Alice?" said Robert's dad. "You weren't too good in the Colosseum."

"Fine, thank you," said Alice.

"Dad doesn't seem too cross that we weren't where we should have been," whispered Robert.

"He's probably just relieved to see us, like parents generally are," said Alice.

"Where did you two go?" snapped Jessica.

Alice groaned.

"You left me out again. It's not fair... "

"Sorry. O.K?" said Alice. "We got lost. It's no big deal!"

"Hmmph!"

Jessica stomped off in front. They walked back to the hotel in silence and went up to their rooms to change.

Alice looked at herself in the fancy gilt mirror hanging on the bedroom wall.

"Umm! Not good!" she said. She had big black circles under her eyes and her long strawberry blond hair was in need of a major brushing to get it smooth. She threw herself on to the bed. Still, she *had* been rescuing ancient British nobility and escaping from violent Roman teenagers. Not bad work really. The problem was, they had to go back again, and try and avoid Agrippina somehow. And it would probably be best done tonight. She'd overheard Robert's parents talking about their early flight on the way back tomorrow. And that reminded her. They were going to have to time travel once they were back in England too, to put the keys back. That didn't sound too difficult though. At least there wouldn't be Britannicus to deal with.

"Umm. Wonder what other nasty little surprises there will be, though," she said to herself. But for now, she needed to find Robert and plan their final journey in Rome.

She sneaked up to the door of the en-suite bathroom. Jessica was absorbed squeezing a spot in the mirror. Alice tiptoed passed and escaped from the bedroom. She tapped on Robert's door.

"Rob! It's me!" she whispered, looking up and down the corridor. "Let me in."

There was the noise of fumbling and Robert's face appeared in the opening. He was brushing his teeth.

"Like the hair," said Alice, admiring the gelled look.

But Robert gave her a "yeah-I-bet" kind of glare.

"No... really! It's cool. And so is the shirt."

Robert disappeared back into his bathroom, frowning at her.

"Just don't tuck it in like my dad does!" called Alice.

Robert re-emerged, pushing his sunglasses into the pocket of his shirt.

"We have to go back in time again," said Alice, looking through Robert's CD collection.

"Yes. But not from in here. Who knows what was standing on this spot two thousand years ago!

We've got to get back to the Forum."

Alice nodded. She was just about to suggest they asked to go for another walk when someone rapped on the door and Mrs Davenport marched in.

"Wish she wouldn't do that," muttered Robert.

"Ah, Alice! Good grief! You're not changed!"

Alice scowled slightly.

" Come along... quickly! It's our last night in Rome. We've got a table booked. Then we've been lucky enough to get the last few tickets for an evening opening at the *Gallery Borghese.*"

"Tonight, Mum?" said Robert, glancing at Alice.

"Yes. Tonight! Lots of wonderful art," said Mrs Davenport. "Bernini... Raphael... Rubens... Caravaggio..."

"Who?" said Alice and Robert together.

Mrs Davenport looked confused.

"Oh. Well the brochure said... "

"That last name... did you say *Caravaggio?* " said Robert, his eyes wide with excitement.

"Yes. I did. Have you heard of him?"

Robert's mother looked surprised.

"Well... yes... sort of. He was quite a good painter, wasn't he?" said Robert.

"Yes. He most certainly was! If you get a move on, we'll all be able to see for ourselves, won't we?"

Mrs Davenport swept back out and slammed the door.

Alice and Robert looked at each other.

"*Quite* good?" said Alice, sarcastically. "I don't think you'd better let *him* hear you say that!"

They both laughed.

"See you in a minute!" said Alice.

She returned to her room and changed back into her dress. She had woken up again now.

19

Six Twenty-Five

The gallery of the Villa Borghese was strangely silent. The small rooms brimmed with treasures. Groups of spellbound tourists drifted through the one-way tour, gawping at the onslaught of beauty. Even Robert was bewitched by the splendour.

But he couldn't resist sticking his tongue out behind the back of the dour-faced curator. Alice stifled a smile. The man's rigid uniform looked out of place against the flowing blue and gold masterpieces on the wall behind him.

"Hey, look at... " Robert coughed, glanced at the curator and lowered his voice. "Look at this hand," he whispered to Alice.

Robert was staring up at a sculpture of a man with rippling muscles and a flowing beard, carrying a very unhappy looking young woman. At the man's feet snapped a three-headed dog. The bewitching sculpture was carved in pure white marble.

"The fingers look as if they really are digging into her thigh. How did someone carve *that* out of a block of stone?" said Robert.

"It's the story of Pluto carrying off the daughter of the Greek goddess Earth into the underworld of Hades," said Alice, reading the English paragraph on the information stand.

"Cool," said Robert, walking around the frozen group. "From this side, you can even see her tears. Who made this then? Michelangelo?"

"No. This was carved in the next century. A sculptor called Bernini."

Robert shrugged and walked on to the next room. Alice lingered a few more minutes, unable to take her eyes from the intricate masterpiece. She turned to have a last look in the doorway, conscious of the cluck of disapproval from the curator.

"Goodbye," she whispered to the sculpture.

"Have you seen anything by *our friend* yet?" said Robert.

"No. But... it says here, they're in the last room... Room VIII," said Alice.

"Come on, then. Let's go straight there," said Robert.

Alice had to skip to keep up with Robert as he wound his way through the next few rooms.

"How are we going to know which paintings are Caravaggio's?" she called.

"Not a problem, I think!" said Robert, stopping abruptly as they entered the last room on the ground floor. "Look!"

Alice gasped. There was Caravaggio looking straight at her from a painting.

"He painted himself!" said Alice.

"That one's his," said Robert, examining the inscription underneath. "And that one, and this... "

"They're smaller than I imagined," said Alice. "And... quite harsh really. But very, very clever. You can't really tell whether he's smiling at us or not, can you?"

"Bit like the *Mona Lisa*, you mean?"

"Sort of. Look... his fingernails are dirty... just like in real life! I think I can see why his work was different from the others at the time. It's more modern... realistic."

"I like this one," said Robert.

"Oh, wow!"

It was a painting of a very old man writing with a

quill. There was a skull on the table beside him.

"Look how shiny his bald head is," said Robert. "It's shinier than the skull. Bit spooky really."

"It's amazing! Nearly 3D! You could almost touch them."

Alice smiled in admiration.

"Can't wait to tell him we've seen these!" she said.

"Not tonight, I think," said Robert, yawning.

Alice frowned.

"What are we going to do, then?"

"I have *got* to sleep," said Robert.

"Tomorrow morning, then. Early. Let's meet in front of the hotel at six o'clock, before the others get up."

Robert looked half-hearted about that suggestion.

"Rob! We've got to!"

"Yeah! Yeah! I know. All right. I'll set my alarm."

Alice nodded. When they got back to the hotel, she fell asleep straight away.

At six the next morning, the alarm on her mobile phone buzzed in Alice's ear from under her pillow like a suffocating wasp. She shot her hand underneath and silenced it, glancing across at Jessica to check her eyes were still shut.

"Urgh!"

She fell back on the pillow. For a short while, she wrestled with the creamy comfort of sleep. The memory of Britannicus and the cruel expression on Agrippina's face buzzed into her consciousness and she awoke with a start. She looked at the time.

"Oh, no!"

It was six twenty-five. She slid into her trousers and picked up her roller boots. One of them slipped. She drew her breath, but managed to catch it just before it hit the marble floor. She swapped one boot into each hand for safety and crept out of the room. Once in the hotel corridor, Alice could breathe more easily. She pulled on her boots and ran down the staircase and out to the early morning streets of Rome.

The city was alive. The traffic scoured the roads as if it had never slept. Alice chuckled as she recognised Robert admiring the bikes and scooters already arranged outside the hire shop.

"You managed to get up then," said Alice walking over to him.

"Ye-es," said Robert, sarcastically tapping his watch. He returned to his inspection. "Hey! Look at that one!"

He squeezed between the outer row of mopeds to a mountain bike propped against the wall. After testing the brake handle, and a furtive glance in the direction of the shop door, Robert slid himself astride the saddle.

"Nice!" he purred.

Alice shook her head hopelessly at him.

"Come on! We've got a quest to finish. Remember?"

Robert grinned at her. But then his expression changed to one of discomfort.

"Oh. I feel grotty," he said.

But Alice already knew. She felt it too.

"Uh, oh! Looks like the keys have decided it's now or never!" she said.

She took a step towards Robert and reached to take his hand. She felt him pull her towards him, on to the cross bar of the bike.

"Ouch . . . !"

Before she could say any more, they were time travelling once again, bumping and spinning through the mother of all spirals, back to a time of emperors and gladiators. And this time, the bike was with them too.

20

𝔄grippina's 𝔕evenge

𝕿he cobbled Twenty First Century slope was now a steep rise of stone steps. The mountain bike tyres bounced down. Alice gripped the middle of the handlebars tighter to keep her sideways balance on the cross bar.

"Hang on!" shouted Robert.

He spat out some of Alice's hair and squeezed on the brakes, dragging his feet on the ground as the bike jerked on to the flat road below. Miraculously, they were still upright but Alice was catapulted off the cross bar with the sudden halt. She collided with a passing soldier.

"Ahh!"

She lunged away from him, as their bodies touched. The soldier tripped and cursed in Latin, looking around for the source of the attack. With a perplexed frown, he walked off, nursing a sore arm.

"That hurt!" said Alice.

Robert was grinning at her.

"It's not funny!"

"It is!" he said. "And having this bike here is really wicked! I think we could have a lot of fun with this!"

He pretended to drive it at a passing cart. The horse, sensing something, snorted and flicked back its ears.

"Ha! Can't see me can you!" mocked Robert. The Roman driver whipped the animal on.

"Shall we try and find that Temple of Vesta then?" said Alice.

"Yep! It was this way."

They walked past the temples and basilicas of the Roman Forum. Robert wheeled the bike.

"Hey! This is the place where Claudius died!" said Robert.

Alice nodded, recognising the doors through which she had skated.

"So, do you think he's dead already?" said Robert. "Last time we were here with Octavia and Britannicus was *before* he died wasn't it?"

"Yes. I think you're right. Now, we're after Claudius was murdered. Yes... of course! I've remembered now!" said Alice.

"Remembered what?" said Robert.

"When we came back here, the very first time... when we saw Claudius dead... do you remember that group of Vestal Virgins that we hid from, as they came out of Claudius' chamber with Agrippina?"

Robert half nodded.

"One of them could see us. Do you remember?" said Alice.

"Oh, yes. You thought you saw her looking at you under her veil," said Robert.

"Yes! Exactly! That was Vittoria... I'm sure now! I bet time *has* passed here, until after Claudius' murder," said Alice.

"She'll be close to Agrippina then?" said Robert.

"Mmm. Unfortunately, I think she will."

They were at the foot of the steps to the Imperial Palace.

They looked at each other.

"After you!" said Robert graciously.

Alice started up the steps and Robert carried the bike. Alice opened one of the double doors. It was still and quiet inside.

"Hold the door open, will you," said Robert.

They edged inside.

"What makes you think we'll find them in here again?" said Robert, almost whispering.

"I didn't say we would. But we may as well start here as anywhere."

They entered the cool interior. Their footsteps and the clicking purr of the bike wheels magnified in the silence. Alice shivered. They reached the inner courtyard. The fountain still babbled peacefully in the centre and this time, there were no guards. Alice crossed to the door and gently pulled it open.

Inside, the couches and tables were tidy. The long cushions and drapes were neatly arranged and a few ornamental bowls decorated the tables in the place of the fatal feast they had seen displayed before.

"You came. How sweet!"

Alice and Robert jumped round. Britannicus was smiling at them from a corner throne. He lounged across the chair with one of his legs draped over a gilded arm.

"You!" said Alice.

"Yes. ME! Little me! Sorry to disappoint you."

Britannicus suddenly leapt from the seat and walked over to them.

"And I knew you would come back for *her*. So did my stepmother!" he sneered.

"Where is she? Where is Vittoria?" said Alice. "She does not belong here."

"Belong? Who of *us* belongs anywhere? We time travellers are all nomads. That is our gift and our curse. I do not belong here. I do not intend to stay. Not now Agrippina has succeeded. She has murdered my father, aided, I am sure, by my thug of a stepbrother. They're all out at the declaration of Nero as Caesar. The ceremony is taking place as we speak. Why do you think it is so quiet around here? My father has only been dead for a few hours and already she orchestrates the final act of her plan! I was always a threat to her, especially because I am a time traveller. So she poisoned my father's mind against me, just as she poisoned his body. How do you think she will treat me now?"

"Well," said Robert. "It doesn't look good, mate!"

Alice frowned at him.

"What do you think Agrippina will do?" she said.

"I do not intend to stay here and find out. I do not ask you to give me a key. But let me come with you. Take me to your time."

Britannicus caressed the handlebars of the mountain bike.

"Your time is so exciting. You have done so much more than us," he said.

"I'm not sure, actually," said Alice. "Your people brought a lot to our land and laid the foundations of our civilization."

Britannicus stared at Alice with his clever brown eyes. Alice felt a flash of warmth. But only for a moment.

"Ha!" sneered Britannicus suddenly. "Flattery will get you nowhere!"

He grabbed Alice viciously and bent both her arms behind her, pulling her away from Robert.

"I *will* come with you!" he shouted.

"O.K! O.K!" said Robert, from the other side of the bike. "If you let her go, we can talk about it."

But Britannicus gripped both Alice's wrists in one hand and felt in one of her many trouser pockets for the key.

"Why do you wear these garments!" he cursed, swapping over and trying the zipped leg pocket on the other side.

"Ah, ha!"

He wrenched the Time Trigger from the pocket.

"Arrhh!" he cried, dropping the key on to the floor. "It burns!"

The Time Trigger rolled across the marble surface towards the entrance of the Roman baths. Robert lowered the bike to the ground and lunged towards it. Just as he was about to pick up the key, a shadow darkened the doorway.

21

Mountain Bikes and Roman Baths

A woman's foot stepped deliberately on to the key. Robert skidded to a stop.

"Agrippina!" breathed Britannicus.

The tall, elegant lady smiled slowly at him with cruel eyes. In silence, she stooped and picked up the Time Trigger. She tossed it gently in her palm and looked from Britannicus to Robert and then at Alice. With raised eyebrows, she studied Alice's baggy trousers, bare waist and roller boots. Alice felt the hairs stand up on the back of her neck. The white chalk painted on Agrippina's face glowed like a mask of evil. When she finally spoke, her voice was harsh and crisp.

"Dear, dear. The centuries have not been kind to fashion," she tutted.

Then she clicked her fingers and a young priestess appeared from behind her.

Agrippina tore back the veil and sneered.

"Vittoria!" said Alice.

"The lions should have finished her the first time," said Agrippina. "They will not fail this afternoon. There will be an exceptional crowd today... the day that my son is made Caesar! I will be... "

Without warning, a shrill alarm pierced the air. Everyone looked towards Robert, startled by the eerie noise.

"Not if I can help it!" said Robert, pushing in a button on his watch.

In a flash, he rammed the mountain bike at Agrippina's stomach sending her flying back through the archway, gasping for breath. He caught the back wheel and rammed her a second time, propelling her into the water of the Roman baths, under a parachute of robes. The bike clattered to the floor and Robert launched himself into the water after her. The splashing sent magnified echoes around the chamber.

Alice jumped round, looking for Britannicus, expecting an attack. But to her surprise, he plunged into the water too. She watched with Vittoria as three bodies writhed in the water, their limbs engulfed in togas and gowns that mushroomed on the surface like oversized lily pads.

Then, like the Lady of the Lake, a hand erupted from the depths of the pool clutching the sparkling Time Trigger, followed by Robert's gasping face.

"Thank goodness!" shouted Alice.

"You shall not have it!" spluttered Britannicus.

He dived towards Robert.

Almost in slow motion, Robert flicked the Time Trigger key high into the air towards Alice and Vittoria.

"Oh... nooo... !" said Alice.

She lunged forward and reached her biggest reach.

The wrestlers, waist high in the bath water, let go of each other and gawped in silence as Alice made a dive that England's rugby team would have been proud of. Her hand grasped the Time Trigger and she slid across the slippery marble, crashing into the mosaic tiles on the far wall of the baths.

The pain of the impact was huge and nagging. She lingered with her face to the wall, unsure what to do next. Then she heard a familiar low clicking sound. She turned, half smiling.

"Well done, Vittoria!" she said.

Vittoria had wheeled over the mountain bike.

At that moment, Alice saw Robert punch out at Britannicus with a violence that surprised her. His clenched fist smashed into the older boy's face with a sickening crack and Britannicus staggered back into the arms of his floundering stepmother.

"Flame! That hurt!" said Robert, clutching his fist.

But it had given him a chance. He plunged towards the side of the pool.

"Here! Take my hand!" said Alice.

Helped by Alice, Robert levered himself out in one final athletic jump, showering everybody with water. He hurdled on to the bike saddle.

"Vittoria! Sit here... quickly!" he shouted.

He stood up on the pedals. Vittoria scooped up her long dress and sat on the saddle, holding Robert's waist. Robert pointed to the metal luggage frame fixed above the rear mudguard.

"Come on, Alice! What are you waiting for?" he said.

"On there?" said Alice.

"Yes. No choice! Now would be good," said Robert.

Alice glanced in the water. Britannicus, wiping blood from his nose, was wading furiously towards them.

"The things I do for... for... someone!" she said.

In two strides, Alice was on the bike. They skidded off around the sides of the Roman bath.

"What monster is that they ride?" said Agrippina, still standing in the water, her soggy hairstyle drooping around her face.

But Britannicus was out of the pool now.

"No! No! Not again! You shall not escape again!" he screamed.

"Oh yes we shall!" yelled Robert over his shoulder.

He cycled furiously, through the archway and across the imperial chamber, crashing into the side of several of the low tables.

"Ow! Ow! Ow!" said Alice. "Do you think you could watch where you're going. It hurts sitting on this thing!"

"Sorry!" said Robert. "I'm doing my best."

"Well do better!"

With some difficulty, Robert steered the bike through the inner courtyard, narrowly missing the side of the fountain, and into the huge, colonnaded ante-room of the palace, just as Alice had done before on her roller boots.

The mountain bike was gaining speed on the polished marble floor. Robert headed for the open door.

"Steps, Rob," said Alice. "STEPS!"

"Use a Time Trigger, Alice!" said Robert. "GET US OUT OF HERE!"

Alice squeezed her fingers around the key. She felt the edges of the ancient disc digging into her hand, but she kept on squeezing.

"Now! Please! Please . . . " she muttered.

She closed her eyes and buried her face in Vittoria's back. Everything went black for the smallest time, then blinding white. Then, a whirl of rainbow colours. And finally, a blue Italian sky.

Instantly, Alice knew they had time travelled, but she had more pressing problems at that moment. The bike had landed with a thud on to thick grass. Alice wasn't sure which was worse, the pain in her bottom from the landing or the certain knowledge that they were headed at great speed towards a very wide column and they were completely out of control. She heard Robert swear.

Alice tried to tip herself off sideways, like falling off skis, and she pulled Vittoria with her, just a fraction of a second before the impact.

Alice sprawled across the grass, rubbing her dazed

118

head. Then, she remembered Robert. She sat up. That hurt even more.

"Rob!"

She dragged herself up on to her knees and crawled over to where Robert lay motionless in the grass at the foot of the column. Vittoria staggered over, nursing a painful looking arm. The bike lay on its side some distance away, its wheels spinning furiously.

"Robert!" said Alice.

She shook him gently with a feeling of dread rising slowly in her stomach.

"Rob," she whispered, bending closer.

22

Mischief

Robert looked dead.

"Don't die on me," said Alice. "I won't have anyone to laugh with... or share secrets with. Please. I'll miss you so much. You're my best friend..."

Vittoria knelt down beside Robert's body.

"Sshhh!" she whispered, putting her finger to her mouth. Alice thought she was almost smiling.

Suddenly, Vittoria lifted Robert's arm and tickled his armpit.

"Oy!" said Robert, opening his eyes and pushing her away.

"You... you... tricker!" said Alice, not sure whether to be annoyed or glad. She punched Robert's arm.

Robert turned to look at her. His blue eyes glinted mischievously and his face creased into a huge grin.

"I'm sorry," he said. "But I couldn't resist. You're a softee, Alice. But... "

"But what?" said Alice.

"But... thanks."

"What for?" said Alice.

She turned and shrugged. She was beginning to feel a bit embarrassed or something.

"For saying what you did," said Robert.

"What did I say? I can't remember now," lied Alice.

"Oh... something about... being best friends and missing me?" said Robert.

"You must have misheard me," said Alice, trying not to look at Robert.

"I don't think so," he said.

Alice looked at Vittoria, hoping desperately that she wasn't blushing. The Italian girl was smiling warmly, her dark, knowing eyes glancing between Robert and Alice.

Someone was coming. Caravaggio was running towards them, shouting in Italian. Alice could hear the sound of horses' hooves not far behind him.

"Quick! This way! They have found me," shouted Caravaggio, switching into English.

Robert dashed over and picked up the bike. He stood on a pedal and scooted it along behind the others, through the ruins of the temple, passed what remained of the side door. They ducked around a corner and into another street. Caravaggio led them on, weaving a trail between the buildings and into a maze of narrow streets, where men on horseback could not follow. They stopped in a cobbled piazza. The beams of wooden balconies hung above them. Dogs and people milled around them. Nobody seemed interested in Caravaggio and Vittoria as they leant against a wall to get their breath back. And no one appeared to notice that they addressed invisible friends in the gap of wall between them.

"You must have done something really bad," panted Alice at Caravaggio.

"Only what I had to," said the young man. "If I cannot work, we cannot eat. Sometimes we have to... borrow."

"Steal?" said Robert, leaning the mountain bike against the wall.

"In this world, if an artist falls ill, or out of favour with the wealthy art-lovers who pay him... then he starves. So we... *borrow*. How else could we buy wine!" He laughed viciously. "And besides, I paint better when I'm drunk! The Vatican guards will never catch *me*. Out here, on the streets, I have many friends. And *they* are not rich hypocrites. But I will play the games of the powerful. For now I will uphold their humour and paint whatever they ask. Then, one day, I will get a chance to pay them back and paint what I really see. That will be my legacy ... the truth."

Alice looked at Caravaggio. She thought he would be capable of worse than stealing if he was provoked. His genius was warped by the cruelty of his youth and his knowledge of other worlds and pain and fear. She was afraid of this enigmatic young man. And yet he had shown a warm love for both his sister and Vittoria.

"Well," said Robert, clearly sensing the tension. "That was fun! But the mission was successful, wouldn't you say? It's all happy families now."

Caravaggio looked at Vittoria and pulled her towards him.

"Yes. Thank you, my friends. We owe you much. But you have one last task ... remember?"

"Ah. That!" said Robert. "Silly me, thinking we could just go home now!"

"But home is exactly where you must go," said Caravaggio. "You must take the three keys back to England with you, and return them to Bardecia."

"By the way," said Alice. "Where's Octavia?"

"Somewhere safe," said Caravaggio.

"Catacombs?" said Robert.

Caravaggio just looked at him.

"Uh, huh!" said Robert. "Bit of a come down after the ol' Temple of Vesta!"

"I don't think she minds," said Alice.

"Only joking!" said Robert.

"Umm. Well getting these keys back through customs might not be such a joke," said Alice.

"Customs?" said Caravaggio.

"Like guards," said Alice.

Caravaggio scowled.

"I'm sure you will think of a way," he said.

Alice looked thoughtfully at the Time Trigger in the palm of her hand.

"How will we find your sister? Where?" she said.

"The same way you found us," said Caravaggio. "The magic of the Time Triggers will guide you, as always. The spirits have chosen you. Bardecia will be there, I feel sure. Somewhere near your home town."

"Newark?" said Robert.

"If that is close to the Fosse Way," said Caravaggio.

"Yes, it is," said Alice. "It's on the Roman road from Lincoln. I know your Roman *friends* passed through there. I've seen the archeological remains of villas in Newark Museum."

"Be careful," said Caravaggio. "There is treachery everywhere."

Alice nodded.

"I think we need to be on our way," said Robert.

He offered Caravaggio his hand. The young painter hesitated for a moment then grasped Robert's arm with both his hands. Vittoria stepped over to Robert and embraced him, kissing his cheek and pausing to look fondly into his eyes. Alice smiled. For the first time ever, she saw Robert blush. Caravaggio took Alice by the shoulders and stared at her.

"Thank you," he said. "You see much, my young friend. I know that. Use your gifts well."

He held her close for several seconds. She smiled back in return, not sure what to say. But she knew that he understood her anyway.

She turned to Vittoria and they hugged each other. A tear was running down Vittoria's scarred cheek.

"You are safe now," said Alice softly.

Vittoria wiped the tear and nodded. But in her eyes, Alice saw that the young Italian woman was not safe here either. She would probably spend the rest of her life haunted by the scars of the gladiator games and trying to cheat starvation and the gallows.

Robert swung his leg over the back of the bike and stood forward so that Alice could sit behind him, on the saddle. She held out the Time Trigger and closed her fingers over it.

"Here! Take this," said Caravaggio, thrusting something into Alice's other hand. "A little souvenir!"

Alice felt the folded paper, but there was no time to look. She stuffed it into her pocket and held tightly around Robert's waist. The whirling of stars and fire was building in her head and through the haze of time travel, she smiled one last time at the fading figures of Caravaggio and Vittoria.

They were back. The buzz and glamour of modern Rome greeted them like an old friend.

"Not bad for a morning's work," said Robert, giving Alice a wink.

"Come on," said Alice. "We'll have to chuck our stuff in the cases... oh... and pretend we've been out shopping or something!"

"Um... I think we'd better put this bike back," said Robert. "The shop is only just over there."

"We didn't deliberately take it," said Alice.

Robert looked at her and grinned. He inspected the sturdy mountain bike and brushed some ancient dust from the mudguard. Alice pulled some grass from between the spokes.

"Only one or two little scratches," said Robert, chuckling. "One adventurous owner! Whoever buys this little beauty will never know just how cool she really is!"

"I'll go and check the coast is clear," said Alice, sauntering off to the front of the shop. She glanced around and waved Robert over.

"Quick!" she said.

Robert carefully slid the bike back among a row of scooters and they both walked away. Robert held up his hand to Alice and she smacked it in triumph.

On the way back to the hotel, Alice unfolded the piece of old paper that Caravaggio had given her.

"Oh! Rob... look!" she gasped.

Robert backtracked and glanced at the drawings.

"Umm. Nice," he said.

"They're beautiful!" said Alice.

On the paper, Caravaggio had made several sketches. They were profiles of young women. A tear trickled down a cheek of one, in which the girl's head was bent in sorrow. There was something familiar in the sketches. In one, she almost saw Octavia's eyes. But another was more like Vittoria. And the hair... a reddish tinge, drawn with a special charcoal... that was very similar to her own.

"I wonder if he used these sketches to do a painting?" said Alice.

"You'll have to look it up in an art book when you get home," said Robert.

Alice nodded as she carefully re-folded the paper and put it securely in her back pocket, smiling to herself. She would keep the sketches safe forever, in her secret box of treasures.

They ran back up the hotel steps and straight into a stack of suitcases. Mrs Davenport glared at them.

23

Smugglers

Jessica sniggered.

"Right!" bawled Mrs Davenport. "You two have nearly made us miss our plane! Robert, you will not get your allowance for the next two months. And as for you, young lady..." She glared at Alice. "I shall be having words with your mother when we get back!"

Robert tried a weak smile at his mother.

"I will not forget, Robert. Don't think that I will!"

"I'll remind you," said Jessica, too low for Mrs Davenport to hear.

But Robert and Alice were close enough. Robert looked up at the ceiling for a second, then casually stepped backwards, standing very heavily on his cousin's sandalled foot.

"Aaah...!"

"I am *so* sorry, Jess!" said Robert, turning suddenly in apparent surprise. He gripped her arm roughly and Alice fancied that he murmured something threatening in Jessica's ear.

"O.K. That's enough," said Robert's father. "Everybody in the taxi. Now!"

With a last glance at his cousin, Robert grabbed the handles of one of the cases and stomped through the sliding doors. The others followed. Alice picked up her own bag. It felt very lumpy. She suspected Jessica had been asked to pack her things and had stuffed everything in any old how.

"Oh, well. No choice," she thought to herself, remembering the excitement of their time travels earlier. She patted her back pocket. She would need to find time to repack her things at the airport. She wanted to slip Caravaggio's drawings into her own sketchbook for safety. And she needed to put the Time Triggers somewhere. She could put them in her soap bag. They would probably be camouflaged with her bracelets and hair stuff. But her big bag would go into the luggage hold on the aeroplane, and somehow she didn't want to be separated from the keys.

The taxi sped through the streets of Rome and Alice took her last look at the chaos and splendour. She would definitely have to return. She had only seen a tiny fraction of the treasures. And she loved the pizzas.

"I'll be back," she whispered through the window.

Alice got a chance to repack her bag on the train to the airport. She emptied it out in the luggage compartment between the carriages. It wasn't easy, balancing and trying to fold her T-shirts while moving out of the way of passengers all the time. She slipped into the toilet cubicle. Sitting on top of the toilet seat, she emptied her purse into her lap. There was a jumble of euros and English currency.

"That'll have to do," she said to herself.

Alice took the Time Trigger keys from a zipped pocket half way down one of her trouser legs. She slipped the larger pendant from its pouch and dropped it with the other key among the coins.

"Camouflage and confidence," she said as she took a deep breath and practiced a smile at herself in the mirror.

When she returned to her seat, Alice opened the zip of her purse and nodded at Robert to look inside.

"What?" he growled. "I don't need you gloating over how much money *you've* got, thank you! Your mum might stop your allowance too."

"Ahem," said Alice, shaking the purse again.

Robert frowned and glanced inside. He was just about to say something unpleasant when he took a second look.

"Oh! I see. Yes. A nice collection of odd coins you have there, Alice. Have another one!" He flipped his own Time Trigger from his key ring and dropped it into the jumble. "Now *put them away!*" he hissed.

He raised one eyebrow before looking casually out of the window.

When they got to the metal detector at customs, Alice tipped the contents of her pockets into the tray and walked through the metal doorway, smiling enthusiastically, despite her racing heartbeat. The customs lady didn't even look in the tray and waved Alice through dismissively. Robert walked through after and winked at Alice.

"You didn't set off the alarms this time then?" sneered Jessica.

"Look, Jess," said Robert, wheeling round. "I'm very sorry that Alice and I left you out a bit, O.K? You know I'm going to pay for that for the next two months without an allowance. Can you drop it? Can we be friends... just for the rest of the journey?"

Jessica scowled and stalked off. Robert shrugged. He nudged Alice as she put her purse back in the leg pocket of her trousers.

"So far, so good!" he whispered.

The flight back to London was fairly uneventful. The highlight was choosing snacks from the refreshment trolley. Alice was grateful for a rest. She listened to the music through the aeroplane stereo system and dozed, dreaming of fantastic mosaics. Then, in her dream, she saw the golden silhouette of Lincoln Minster shining in the sunlight. The castle squatted on its mound beside it.

"It's Lincoln, Rob," she said, sitting up suddenly.

"Pardon?" said Robert.

"I think we have to take the keys back to Lincoln," said Alice. "Near the cathedral somewhere."

Robert raised his eyebrows.

"You think?" he said.

"Yes. I do. It's worth a try isn't it? Caravaggio called the thing they came from the *Lindum Shield*, didn't he? Well *Lindum* is the Roman name for Lincoln."

"I know that!" said Robert.

"Well, shall we see if we can go for the day on the train?" said Alice.

"Mmm. You'd better give me a few days with Mum to soften her up!" said Robert.

Just then, the Captain lowered the aeroplane wheels ready for landing and Alice closed her eyes and gritted her teeth. She really didn't like the take off and landing bit of flying.

Alice's mum was at the airport to meet them, which was wonderful. All the way back home, Alice chatted wildly about Rome.

"You really do seem to have seen a lot," said her mother, obviously impressed with the detail that Alice used to describe the imperial buildings and the original decoration of the dome in St. Peter's.

"Yes. We certainly did a lot of *travelling* when we were there," said Alice, smiling to herself.

But the quest was not over yet.

24

The Train to Lincoln

Alice was really pleased to see Sarah and her other school friends again. At break time, she managed to meet Robert near the P.E. shed without causing any comment.

"Did your mum agree to the train then?"

"Haven't dare ask, yet. She's still in a mood! But I think she will."

Alice offered him a carrot stick from her snack.

"You do bring some weird things to eat for break," said Robert, shaking his head. "What's wrong with crisps?"

"I like carrots," said Alice, pretending to be offended. "And nuts. And cherry tomatoes!"

"Yuk," said Robert.

"Gotta go," said Alice. "People will talk."

Robert smiled at Alice and ran off.

"Meet you tomorrow for the twelve o'clock train from Newark Castle station, unless I tell you otherwise," he called back.

Alice nodded. Twelve o'clock sounded late enough on a Saturday for a decent lie-in.

At five minutes to twelve the next morning, Alice's mum dropped her off near Newark Castle, just in time for her to run through the gap from the car park on to the platform before she heard the wooing sound of the level crossing barriers going down. The Nottingham to Lincoln train approached Newark station. She breathed a sigh of relief when she spotted Robert.

"You made it then," said Alice, as they boarded the

little train.

"No sweat," said Robert, taking off his hoody and dumping it on the seat next to him.

They paid the conductor their one pound sixty-seven.

"Are the Time Triggers safe?" said Robert.

"Yep! Never left my side," said Alice. "Oh, by the way... I looked up paintings by Caravaggio in the school library and... guess what?"

"What?"

"He *did* paint the sketches... my sketches. Look!"

Alice pulled a notebook from her little rucksack and opened the cover. Inside was a photocopy of a painting.

"*Repentant Magdalene*," read Robert. "Caravaggio's first painting of a woman, done in 1596. Ah, ha! Hey... she looks a bit like you. Funny that!"

"She doesn't! Vittoria more like!" said Alice.

Alice put it away carefully.

"It's in some gallery in Rome," she said. "I'll go back one day and have a look at the real thing."

"So, what's the plan for today, then?" said Robert.

"Well, I've been doing a bit of research about Roman Lincoln this week."

Robert looked at her admiringly.

"I've been busy with the football team practices," he said. "And we've had *loads* of homework. I don't know how you get the time to waste in the library!"

"Oh, I did most of it at home on the net," said Alice.

"Oh." Robert looked a little guilty. "And... ?"

"Well, Lincoln was once a big Roman fortress. A sort of headquarters for the Ninth Legion in this area. And this part of England *was* the territory of the Corieltauvi Tribe... which we knew anyway. But the Romans weren't always violent. Lots of them settled and mixed with the tribes and built

131

villas and roads and towns."

"Sort of immigrants then?" said Robert.

"Yes. I suppose so," said Alice. "Anyway, I wanted to tell you, I saw a photo of a shield on the net. It wasn't all that clear, but the circular shapes decorating it looked awfully like our keys."

"And where is this shield now?" said Robert.

"In a museum in London," said Alice. "It was found near the mound under Lincoln Castle. Apparently there could be loads of archeological treasures still buried there. But... and this is the interesting part... the shield went missing a few weeks ago and the police have never been able to work out how it was stolen. No trace of a break-in. But it did happen the day before a mini earth tremor."

"Ah, ha! Now there's a coincidence!" said Robert.

"Exactly! I reckon it wasn't stolen. I think it vanished because we're about to have a Time Crash, like Caravaggio said... unless *we* get these keys back to Roman Lincoln! The complete shield won't exist to be discovered if we don't, and neither will we!"

At that moment, the train pulled into Lincoln Station. Robert and Alice got off and walked through the town centre and up Steep Hill towards the castle.

"Look. I want to show you something," said Alice at the top of the hill. They walked a little bit further into Bailgate.

"Do you see these round things in the middle of the road... what do you think they are?" she asked Robert, pointing to the line of odd looking bricks laid in circles along the pretty street.

"Drains? Man hole covers?" said Robert.

Alice shook her head.

"They're the base of *real* Roman columns! This was a colonnaded forum two thousand years ago, with a basilica and a temple and baths and everything!"

"I never noticed these before," said Robert. "Cool! Hey, look at that sweet shop!"

Alice glanced at the shop window. She wanted to tell Robert more about things, but the jars of sweets did look very interesting. They went inside and spent a few minutes choosing two varieties each. Alice decided on the apple shaped ones and American hard gums.

"Right then," said Robert, once they were back outside. "Let's get on with it."

They stood together at the side of the Newport Arch.

"If we go back here, we'll be just inside the North Gate of the fortress," said Alice, passing a key to Robert.

Robert nodded, and as they had done so often now, they concentrated their thoughts on their power to time travel. The magic of the Time Triggers surged through their bodies.

Alice opened her eyes and released her grip on her coin-shaped key.

"Wow! We did it!" said Alice.

"Wicked!" said Robert.

They were inside a bustling Roman fortress. Carts and people milled everywhere. It was dirty and noisy and smelly.

"Hey... it's very similar to Ancient Rome," said Alice, with the conviction of someone who really did know.

"Let's try this way," said Robert, brushing past citizens and soldiers as he walked through the arched gate.

"The road here is way lower than in our time," said Alice. "It's been gradually buried over the centuries. No wonder the remains of street cobbles and mosaic floors are buried down in the cellars of the modern shops in the Twenty First Century."

"Concentrate, will you," said Robert. "Somehow, we've got to find Caravaggio's other sister among all these people. Alice... ?"

Alice had stopped. She froze in horror. In between the other people from a bygone age who were oblivious to the presence of the two time travellers, one person was looking directly at them.

"You again!" said Robert. "I thought you were in Rome. I thought you got murdered!"

"Sorry to disappoint you, my friends," said the Roman centurion, drawing his sword.

25

A Last Surprise

Britannicus laughed at them.

"Aren't you going to shout for your soldier friends?" said Robert unpleasantly. He pointed to a unit of legionaries marching past.

"If I want a job doing, it seems that I must do it myself," said Britannicus.

Alice and Robert had their backs against the arch wall. The red feathers of Britannicus' helmet bristled in the breeze.

"Your weather in this land is bad," he said. He pulled his cloak closer, over his woollen tunic and breastplate. "And the food... we have had to teach you much!"

"Why don't you go back to Rome then?" said Robert.

"No can do, I'm afraid. I've died there once already!"

"What do you mean?" said Alice.

"Well, *I* haven't. But Agrippina and dearest Nero think I have," said Britannicus. "Some poor slave took my place. I escaped with the army and spent a long time travelling, until finally, I reached Britain. Rather fitting, don't you think? This land gave me my name after all!"

"Why here? Why not some other warmer part of your empire?" said Robert.

"Do you mean Gaul? Or Greece?" said Britannicus.

"Yes, anywhere! Why Britain?" said Robert.

"Because of you two, you fools!"

"Oh, I get it," said Robert. "You want the keys!

You came all this way to get your hands on the Time Triggers." Robert laughed. "Then *you* are the fool!" Despite being pinned to the wall by the blade of a Roman sword, Robert started giggling. "*You* can't use the Time Triggers any more! You burnt your bridges, mate, when you messed about going forwards in time, just like Caravaggio. That's why it hurt when you tried to pick them up."

Britannicus scowled. Then, to Alice's surprise, he lowered the weapon and smiled at them.

"I know," he said softly.

"Then... why... I don't understand," said Robert.

"I fell in love," said Britannicus.

Robert and Alice looked at him in stunned silence.

"In *love*?" said Alice, eventually. "With whom?"

"With me," said a pretty young woman, stepping out of the shadow of the archway.

"And *you* are... ?" said Robert sarcastically.

"I think I know," said Alice, smiling. "You look like your brother."

The young woman nodded.

"Yes. You do know. My name is Bardecia of the Corieltauvi. Britannicus has told me everything. I know that you have met my brother and sister and that you helped them to escape to a new life. I thank you for that from the depths of my heart."

"Then... pardon me for being a little bit on the stupid side here... but why on earth are you trusting this guy?" said Robert. "He wanted to kill them!"

"Not me!" said Britannicus. "I never said I would kill you or anyone else. All I wanted was a key to escape from my murderous stepmother and her spawn. May the gods save Rome, is all I can say! With Nero on the throne, anything is possible! I heard rumours recently, that he set fire to our great city just to make way for a new palace. Doesn't

136

surprise me!"

Alice and Robert looked at one another. Robert was shaking his head.

"You trust *him*, Bardecia? Rubbish! No way! I'm sorry," he said.

"I do, Robert," she said, pushing her thick, red hair behind her shoulders. "I know why he came. And now... yes, I do trust him. He told me about travelling forwards and feeling the keys' power as heat afterwards. I told him what that must mean. I have suspected that after several forward journeys a time traveller would lose their power, from tales the elders used to tell. Anyway, Britannicus could have killed me. But he did not. We... fell in love."

Bardecia looked at Britannicus and in that moment, Alice knew that they spoke the truth.

"Ahh! How sweet!" said Robert, shaking his head. "This is just another trick... "

Without any warning, he punched Britannicus on the jaw. As the Roman spluttered backwards, Robert twisted the short, powerful sword from Britannicus' hand and pushed him to the floor.

"No!" cried both Bardecia and Alice together, as Robert pinned Britannicus against the cobbles with his foot, wielding the sword menacingly, near to the Roman's face.

Britannicus lay still, staring fearlessly into Robert's eyes.

"Kill me if you wish," he said. "But tell me this, young friend, do you wish to leave my heir without a father?"

Robert frowned and he and Alice looked at Bardecia, who nodded.

"We are married and yes, I am pregnant. Our child will grow up to be a great leader here in Britain who will bring together our peoples. The legionaries do not know Britannicus' true identity, and never will. That life is ended. He is just a brave centurion who has been granted release from the army to join me at a settlement to the South West of here. We have begun construction of a large villa from where we can look after my people. Not all Romans are bad, you know. There are many others like Britannicus, who just want peace and prosperity. And with all that we both know as time travellers, there is so much good that we can do."

"And bad!" snorted Robert.

"Why? Why would I? What have I got to gain?" said Britannicus from beneath the point of Robert's sword.

"He's right," said Alice. "I believe them."

"And what of the keys then?" said Robert.

"We must put them back in the Lindum Shield where they belong," said Bardecia. "Once they are safely back, they will lose their power as Time Triggers and the true timeline will be restored."

Robert looked uncertainly at Alice. She nodded at him.

"I think Bardecia is right," she said.

"*Think?*" said Robert.

"O.K. I know."

Robert took a deep breath and exhaled slowly, looking at Britannicus down the length of the shiny blade.

26

The Lindum Shield

Robert lowered the sword and stepped back next to Alice. For a moment, no one moved. It was Alice who broke the silent spell. She offered Britannicus her hand. A friendly smile spread across the young man's face and he clasped her wrist, pulling himself up from the ground. He brushed the dirt from his cloak and tunic.

"Come," he said, heading off down the hill. "Keep the sword if you feel more comfortable," he added to Robert.

They followed him through the northern suburbs of Roman Lincoln. It was a vibrant, bustling community where Britons mixed with Romans to trade, learn crafts and drink wine.

Eventually, they entered a dwelling. The inside was neatly furnished with low chairs and tables and elegant pottery. Bardecia gestured to them to sit down.

"Don't eat or drink anything," hissed Robert under his breath. "These people love poisons, remember!"

Bardecia opened a double-fronted, wooden cabinet that stood on a high table against the wall. It was elaborately carved and inlaid with jewels. She removed something and placed it on the table in front of them. She gently unwrapped the protective cloth.

"The Lindum Shield," she said, revealing the finely engraved iron rectangle, about the size of a large book. Down the centre were three round, empty holes.

Alice felt dizzy and breathless with a sudden rush

of power. She looked at Robert, and then at the other two, and knew that they all felt it. There was a magical energy between them all. She reached down to her trouser leg pocket and undid the zip. Feeling very short of breath, and with her heart thumping inside her, she carefully put the two Time Trigger keys on the table beside the shield. Robert put his one next to them. In the silence, Alice sensed the knowledge that what they were about to do was right and good.

"We will keep it safe, among the treasures of our people," said Bardecia.

"I've just remembered... " said Alice. "We will need to get back to our own time."

"Oh! I never thought of that! Is it possible without the keys?" said Bardecia.

"Well, last time we... "

"You have returned Time Triggers somewhere else already?" asked Britannicus in surprise.

Alice and Robert both nodded. Britannicus raised his eyebrows and smiled in admiration.

"As I was saying," continued Alice. "... we had to take something... anything... from the age to which we had travelled, and touch it on a Time Trigger. That gave us just enough energy to get home."

"Right, then," said Bardecia, smiling and looking around. "See anything that takes your fancy?"

Robert looked down at the Roman sword with interest.

"Another sword?" said Alice.

"Oh, yes!" said Robert, gently running his fingers along the smooth blade. "It should look good on my bedroom wall next to the French medieval one." He looked across at Britannicus for approval.

"Take it, my friend," said the young Roman.

"What about this for you, Alice... ' said Bardecia.

She reached into the wooden cabinet and took out a delicate golden chalice marked with ancient engravings. Alice's blue eyes sparkled. She was speechless.

"Please, I insist," said Bardecia. "In some ways, it belongs to you. You are our descendent after all."

Alice took the cup with pride.

"Right, then," said Robert. "Time to go, I think. No offence or anything!"

He looked across at Alice and pointed to the Keys of Rome. She nodded. With a trembling hand, she picked one up for the last time. Robert did the same. Bardecia picked up the third.

The young woman deftly placed the slightly larger key into the central hollow. It fitted exactly. She sat back and took Britannicus' hand.

"Farewell, my friends," said Britannicus. "I trust you will enjoy reading about me in the historical volumes of your time. Somehow, I doubt the scribes will get it right!" He laughed and smiled at them.

Robert nodded respectfully at Britannicus and then at Bardecia.

"Goodbye!" she said.

"Perhaps we shall meet again?" said Alice.

"I think not," said Bardecia. "But perhaps you will visit our villa, near Ad Pontem, or what remains of it in your time! You will know it by the wall painting of the god Cupid we have designed for the baths."

"I'll look for it when we get home," said Alice. "Actually, cupid rings a bell. I've read something... somewhere... in Southwell?"

"Possibly," said Bardecia, shrugging. "I do not know this town. But I should think it is yet to develop during the centuries between us."

Robert held Alice's hand. He bent over and put his key in the hole at the bottom of the shield. It clicked perfectly into place. For a moment, the disc of metal glowed white. Robert touched the blade of his sword against it.

"Wicked!" he said. "Amazing feeling!"

Then Alice gently fitted the last Time Trigger into its rightful resting place in the space at the top of the shield. As if by magic, it seemed to rotate all by itself, until, like the other keys, it clicked comfortably in. Once again, it shone and sparkled with a clear white light. Alice put the side of the beautiful chalice against the Time Trigger.

"Goodbye!" she said to Bardecia and Britannicus.

The immense surge of power enveloped her in a chocolatey embrace, soaking her senses with ultimate knowledge. She flopped against the grassy mound behind her and stared at the sky. She was drained of energy.

"The end of a quest," she said.

Robert turned his head to look at her. He was breathing rapidly.

"Until the next time," he said.

"Do you think there will be a next time?"

"I hope so!" said Robert. "I suppose we'll just have to wait and see if any more Time Triggers turn up. Wouldn't mind a journey back in Egypt!"

Alice grinned. They lay back on the grass in silence. Alice held up her chalice and turned it slowly in her hands. It glittered in the sunlight.

"You were right," said Robert.

"What about?"

"Trusting Britannicus."

"Umm. Do you think they did build a villa somewhere with a painting of Cupid?" said Alice, looking back up at the sky.

"We could always go to the library in the town centre and see if they've got any stuff on local archeology," said Robert.

Alice sat up.

"Come on then!" she said. "Oh! We're here ... "

"Yes. I think you'll find we're always *here*," said Robert sarcastically.

"Oh, you know what I mean! We're by the castle. I wonder what treasures still lie undiscovered beneath us?"

"The Lindum Shield was excavated somewhere near here a few years ago, wasn't it?" said Robert.

"Hey ... I bet we'll find it's back in a London museum now," said Alice. "We've restored the timeline, remember? No more little earthquakes, I think."

Robert nodded.

"Pity we're at the top of the hill," he said. "There's a café that sells great hot chocolate and frozen yoghurt drinks down in the shopping centre, near the station."

"Oh well ... it's down hill all the way," said Alice as she stood up. "Beat you there ... !"

They raced off together, on a different kind of quest.

Acknowledgements

This story is based upon some real historical characters from different periods in history, in particular Britannicus, whose father, Claudius, was the emperor of Rome 41-54 A.D. and the great Italian Renaissance painter, Caravaggio. I have spent many hours researching the lives and times of these people and I owe much to the published work of historians, too numerous to list here. I have sought to keep as true to historical fact as possible but this is a work of fiction and I have, at times, used artistic licence to invent my own theories where history remains vague. However, in the event of time travel, who knows what may be possible!

My special thanks to Richard Joseph for his knowledge, enthusiasm and humour; to Ian Ward, once again, for his exquisite cover painting; to the team at Headland Multimedia for I.T. support; to all the booksellers, teachers, librarians and journalists who have been so supportive; to the talented editors and designers who have worked with the team at Dragonheart; to Emily and Lizzie for their endless inspiration and to my wonderful parents, for a lifetime of love that has made all that I do possible. And finally, an infinity of thanks to my husband, Richard, for being the best of best friends, always. To him this book is dedicated.

L.D.